A LIFETIME *of*

Love

Is Not Enough

A LIFETIME *of*

Love

Is Not Enough

JANE FARABEE

iUniverse, Inc.
Bloomington

A Lifetime of Love Is Not Enough

iUniverse books may be ordered through booksellers or by contacting:

iUniverse
1663 Liberty Drive
Bloomington, IN 47403
www.iuniverse.com
1-800-Authors (1-800-288-4677)

ISBN: 978-1-4759-1104-6 (sc)
ISBN: 978-1-4759-1105-3 (ebk)

Printed in the United States of America

iUniverse rev. date: 05/16/2012

CHAPTER 1

I've heard it all my life and yet still I cringe when people tell me how cute my freckles are. After a few hours in the sun they seem to be waving bright red flags to draw even more attention to them. Now as I gaze at my reflection in the mirror the freckles I had always hoped to grow out of seemed to be multiplying as I tried to cover them with a bit of makeup. After just a few hours in the sun, they seemed to be waving bright red flags, drawing even more attention to them. Rubbing some concealer over them I was not getting the desired effect and decided to give it a break by doing something with my hair.

With two hands full of red kinky hair I was trying different styles, when I heard "damn!" loud and clear from the other room.

"What?" I gasped, almost falling as I ran across our tiny but crowded apartment.

When I got to the bedroom, I was relieved to discover all was well. The sight of my roommate Karen bouncing around as she tried to wiggle out of her tight jeans had me laughing uncontrollably. Of course when she got a look at my face she had her own reason to laugh.

"Lynn, what have you done to yourself?" she laughed as she pointed to the mirror on the dresser.

Her laughter made me self conscious and a bit on edge. One look to the mirror and I saw what she meant. My red hair was sticking far out on both sides, makeup spread thickly over my cheeks. Place a big red nose in the middle and the image will be complete.

I couldn't keep from laughing at the sight of my roommate Karen as she tripped around the room attempting to pull her pants off. She was mumbling some obscenity as she bounced around the room. Finally she fell onto the bed where I grabbed a pant leg. A quick tug freed her from the tight jeans.

"The zipper on my jeans broke." She wined as she got up and headed toward the closet. "They were my last clean pair and I can't go on a hay ride in dirty jeans."

"Calm down, there has got to be a pair in there somewhere." I watched as she tossed clothes on and around the bed in her search. She had found a pair and was pulling them on when I warned. "Hurry up they'll be here any minute."

"Don't nag Lynn," she laughed "or I'll have to start calling you mother." She had quickly pulled on her jeans and was adding to the pile of clothes on the bed in her search for a pair of boot socks when the doorbell rang.

"See right on time as usual," I said handing her a pair of socks from where else but the sock drawer.

I quickly washed my face and put my hair into a pony tail before going to the door. When I opened it Carl stood there looking as handsome as ever. To say the least we made an interesting couple; him with his wavy black hair, chiseled face. His taut lean body with a golden tan had every girl at school determined to make him her own. I on the other hand was cursed with uncontrollable red hair, a slightly overweight body, and my pale face was totally covered with freckles. Still, he loves telling them how I'm the only girl for him. Of course this makes them drool even more . . . gorgeous and faithful.

We met our freshman year and have been going out for almost 3 years now. Behind him was Frank, whose boyish charm, blond hair and smiling blue eyes make him quite handsome despite his oversized ears and large nose that dominate his face.

"Come in and have a seat." I motioned toward the sofa. "Karen will be ready soon." Upon entering Carl gave me a quick hug and a quick kiss on the cheek, while Frank inhaled deeply and smiled.

"What a wonderful aroma." Frank, unlike Carl always noticed such things. "Very sensual," He inhaled deeply again "who has the new perfume?"

"Isn't it wonderful? It's called All Night." Flattered he had noticed I leaned closer so he could get a better whiff. Suddenly pulling back and I grabbed Carl by his belt loop as he passed. "Wait a minute are you wearing jeans?" I couldn't believe what I was seeing." Since when do you even own a pair?"

"What you don't like the new look?" Carl took a manly stance then turned about as if at a fashion show.

"They look great on you." I laughed through a whistle.

Just then Karen burst into the room with her overwhelming energy and zest for life. She's the only one I know who looks absolutely stunning in a pair of jeans and a T-shirt. She tied a red bandanna in her silky auburn hair and began ushering us toward the door. "Come on let's get going," she commanded as if she had been waiting on us rather than the other way around.

Carl was designated driver for the evening so we piled into his green Honda civic. It was not the kind of car he would have picked out for himself. His parents had good intentions when they bought it as a graduation present. We take turns being designated driver, however not being much of a drinker I often volunteer to drive home.

We left the Houston city limits and an hour later we pulled through a gate in need of some repairs. It was so rusty it looked as if a light breeze would make it fall. Letters across the top spelling out Harper Ranch to assure us we were at the right place.

I noticed Paul and Susan coming down the road behind us. By the careless way Paul maneuvered his fiery red mustang, I could tell he had already been drinking heavily.

His hands tight on the wheel and glassy eyes staring out the windshield he zipped past just as we neared the farmhouse. With rocks flying he finally spun the car sideways and came to a stop just inches from a huge pile of hay. Paul got out all smiles howling to his buddies while Susan looked quite piqued. These outings would be a lot more enjoyable without Paul's antics, but Susan has been my friend since we met in high school and for now they came as a pair.

"He's going to get someone killed." Carl said thorough clenched teeth attempting to control his distaste for Paul.

"Hopefully it won't be Susan." I added, "If he won't let her drive home we'll insist she ride with us." I looked to Carl who agreed.

"That'll go over like a lead balloon." Frank commented.

"Maybe we can get his keys and then convince him he lost them on the ride." Karen suggested.

"Great then we'll have to listen to his big mouth for the entire ride home." Carl groaned as his eyes narrowed and the muscles of his jaw drew tight.

"Better than attending his funeral," Frank sighed, "besides he'll probably pass out for most of the ride."

We quickly joined the rest of the group and found Paul had not been the only one to start drinking early. This had sounded like a great idea last month but I was beginning to wish we had opted for a simple dinner and movie.

Our group of twelve, made up of acquaintances from the university and their friends were here for the combination hay ride-cookout. The price was about the same a steak dinner in the restaurants around town, a real bargain. The ranch workers would cook up the food while we were on the ride and then would clean up afterwards. They also offered the meal with a ride on horseback but it would be hard enough to keep this group in a wagon let alone on horseback.

We climbed onto the wagon and made ourselves as comfortable as we could on the hay. I decided to pass as everyone else took a beer from a cooler that had been placed in the middle of the wagon.

As we started the ride there were some purple flowers swaying in the wind. As I watched them I decided purple was actually my favorite color. Oh not to wear, or be owned as on a car but simply to be enjoyed for only the flowers could do justice to such a color.

Paul and his buddies were ready to moon anyone we passed. So it was a good thing we were on private property following a trail through a thick grove of oak and pecan trees. It was really hard to believe these boys would soon graduate from college.

The sun started to sink behind the hills and the temperature dropped quickly. We had brought jackets however they were still in the car. The wagon driver provided blankets and we wrapped them around us. We cuddled close together under them.

As we neared the end of our ride, stars began to show themselves through the canopy of trees. The welcoming glow of a campfire and the aroma of the searing steaks greeted us. We could almost taste them as we got our jackets from the car.

After retrieving them we ate our meal quickly at the picnic table. One by one we made our way over to the campfire as we finished our meal. It was getting colder as we huddled close to the fire as we roasted marshmallows for dessert.

We relaxed as we watched fireflies dance in the trees: trees that seemed to be doing an eerie dance of their own in the glow of the fire.

The splendor of the full moon made it light enough for us to see a group of deer as they came out to feed. Everyone was in awe and being very quiet. I could hear the crackle of the fire until Paul broke the silence. With beer in hand he almost tumbled into the fire. "This is a true story." He laughed.

"Yeah sure it is." Someone taunted.

"Honest." Paul crossed his heart as a child would. He steadied himself then started his story. "There was this American soldier who had been specially trained to sneak up on the enemy at night. He would sneak up on the camp with only the glow of their fire to see by then he would cut and slash until all were dead.

The report says an enemy soldier was trying to surrender but the American just smiled at the man. With one swing of a sword chopped the guy's head off. They say it happened so fast the soldier was able to spit in the fucker's eyes before they closed and his head rolled off.

The girl's groaned while the guys encouraged Paul to tell the rest of the story.

When the war was over they brought the guy home. He thought he was still out there on maneuvers so they put him in the psych ward for years. It was years before he got out. They found him a job as a janitor in small town. He was doing real good until one night the local high school had a bon fire for homecoming.

It was dark when this guy drove by and all he could see were silhouettes around the fire. He snapped killed twenty people and was about to kill number twenty-one.

They say it was young girl kneeling in front of him. She was praying and pleading for her life when he stopped mid-swing. He blinked his eyes and shook his head as if awakening from a dream. He took a step back and looked around at what he had done. He looked at the girl before him, screamed no then ran off into the woods still clutching the knife. There was a huge manhunt but he was never found. Some think he realized what he had done, went off somewhere and killed himself, however others think he is still living out there in the woods," Paul peered off into the darkness, "just waiting to strike again."

It was a new spin on an old tale yet it was still effective.

After Paul's tale everyone got ready to head home.

I don't know how he did it but Carl had managed to get Paul's keys and much to his delight they rode home with another couple. We put the keys in the trunk of Paul's car and I couldn't help wonder if he'd even remember he had never opened it.

I was glad Carl had quit drinking early and was able to drive home. These country roads are narrow and very dangerous at night. The clock on the dash read 2:02 am when we got back to the apartment. All of us were stretching and yawning barely able to keep our eyes open.

Carl and Frank walked us to the door, insisting they didn't want anything to happen to their best girls. I invited them in for coffee but it was late and they needed to get home.

Carl winked with a familiar grin, gave me a kiss goodnight and assured me he would be in touch to make plans for our next big date. How could anyone not love this man? I thought to myself as I closed the door behind me.

I went into the kitchen where Karen was already filling the kettle with water.

"Where are the boys?" she asked placing the kettle on the stove then reaching to turn on the burner.

I walked up behind her and slipped my arms around her waist, as I did she lean back bringing her body closer to mine. "They couldn't stay," I informed her as I lightly kissed the back of the neck. "Maybe we should skip the coffee."

She turned and we embraced eagerly. Then after a full and longing kiss we searched each other's eyes and smiled. "I enjoyed the evening but wish we didn't have to hide all the time. We keep playing these silly games just to be accepted by our friends and classmates." I sighed "I know Carl and Frank enjoy playing our straight dates but one of these nights someone's going to notice who is holding whose hand on these moonlit outings. It could be very hard to explain."

"What's so hard about the truth?" Karen asked.

"People don't want the truth. They'd rather go through life pretending we don't exist."

"I guess you're right," she said.

"They seem to think all gays and lesbians are out to destroy the family unit when nothing could be farther from the truth."

"Enough talk," She said as she took my hand and led me toward the bedroom. "Let's call it a night." Her devilish grin assured me she had planned a long night with very little sleep.

With a smile of my own I followed willingly.

Chapter 2

Awakened by a gentle tapping, I slowly opened one eye then the other. I cursed the interruption yet was unable to make myself move. My eye lids slowly closed and I was soon drifting back into the wonderful world of dreams. Something seemed terribly wrong; I was no longer in the peaceful place I had just left, now I was trembling, kneeling in front of a Marine in his dress blues. In his right hand was a huge knife.

It was long, sharp and glistened in the glow of a fire. I could feel the rush of air as it neared my neck, the sharpness as it touched my skin. If the persistent pounding at the door had not pulled me from my dream, I would surely have lost my head.

So vivid was the dream that when I sat up, my hands immediately went up to my neck. I'm not sure if I were checking for a wound or trying to catch my head. I was short of breath and grateful to have been pulled from this dream.

I groggily pulled myself from the bed and stumbled around looking for my robe. By the glow of the nightlight I smiled at the sight of Karen's sweet face as she continued to dream peacefully.

My desire for her was strong and I probably would have awakened her with a kiss if the tapping hadn't drawn me away. I found my robe and slipped it on as I headed for the door. This time there was a loud knock.

"I'm coming." I called trying to be quite enough not to wake Karen yet loud enough to be heard by whomever was at the door.

I had no idea who it could be but knew it had better be important. I looked through the peephole and was surprised to see Susan pacing back and forth. I opened the door so quickly it startled her.

"What's wrong?" I sounded almost as frantic as she appeared.

"What makes you think anything's wrong?" she hesitated.

"There has to be something or you would not be pacing back and forth in front of my door at . . ." I stopped short and asked. "What time is it anyway?"

"I'm sorry" she was in tears. "I know I shouldn't have bothered you at this hour. I'll just come back later."

I caught her by the arm as she turned to go. "Nonsense that's what friends are for. Now get in here and tell me what's up while I make us some coffee."

"I don't know where to begin," she said sheepishly as she followed me toward the kitchen "It's just I do feel like a caged animal or at least one who is about to be."

I had no idea what she was talking about but knew she would tell in her own time. I turned the burner on under the pot of water Karen had placed there earlier.

"Paul and I had a fight," she said quickly.

"Big surprise." I quipped then immediately wished I could retrieve the words before they reached her ears. "I'm sorry, I didn't mean it."

"Yes you did." Her voice was as cold as her icy stare. I was so sure she would leave and never forgive me that I was surprised when she continued. "Sad thing is I know you're right. We do fight a lot." Her eyes glazed over as she drifted into deep thought for a moment.

"Anyway this time he wants me to give up my education to marry him as soon as he graduates."

"And you don't want to?" I questioned.

"Does it surprise you?" she smiled.

"We have known each other along time and you are constantly talking about being a wife and a mother, so yes it does kind of surprise me."

"I know" she said sheepishly "It is what everyone expects. We've been dating since High School and after six years it does seem to be the next step." After a moment's hesitation she continued, "Actually I'm terribly undecided; a part of me feels obligated to say yes, and yet another part definitely says no."

"I believe when you think about what you're saying you will find the answer." I almost laughed.

She seemed puzzled as she tried to recall what it was she had said. "What do you mean?" she finally asked.

"You say part of you wants to marry Paul, not out of love but out of some sense of obligation while the other part doesn't want to marry him because in your own words you would feel like a caged animal, trapped for the rest of your life."

Susan thought for a moment then said with a slight laugh "I did say that didn't I?"

"Yes, and you're the one who has to live with the decision so you shouldn't worry about what others think. Now here's your coffee and be careful it's hot." I said as I placed the steaming cup on the table in front of her.

She picked up the cup and cautiously sipped from it as she sat back in her chair. We sat in silence and I could see the tension drain from her body. Although she didn't say, I believe she had made her decision.

Karen still wiping the sleep from her eyes came into the room. I was unaware of her presence until I felt her arm slip around my waist.

"Coffee smells good. I'll think I'll have a cup this morning babe." She said with a yawn.

"Karen we have a guest." My heart nearly jumped from my chest as I became rigid and self=conscious with the fear at having been found out.

When Karen realized what I had said her eyes opened wide as her face turned pale then red to match my own.

Susan's face didn't show the shock and horror I had always expected to see when she found out. Instead there was a momentary look of confusion followed by what appeared to be humor as her smile widened.

"I've always suspected you two were more than friends." She laughed.

"You should see the look of panic on your faces. I wish I had a camera."

"It doesn't bother you?" I asked hesitantly, my heart still pounding with the uncertainty of it all.

"Why should it bother me, I think you make a great couple and it does explain some of the things I thought I had noticed before."

Karen looked in my direction seeking some assurance she was hearing correctly and then thanked Susan for her comment.

"I have wanted to tell you so many times over the years but held back because I was sure you wouldn't want to be my friend anymore." I said still surprised by her reaction.

"I know what you mean." She said, "I've had similar reactions when people find out my uncle is gay. It's as if they think it's contagious. They can't get away fast enough."

"You never told me." I accused.

"And you never told me." She repeated my words then looked at me with a warm smile. "Like you I didn't want to lose another friend."

"Touché then you understand why we go to such lengths to keep it secret and will help us keep it that way?" I hated to ask but had to know what to expect.

"They say people choose to be gay." She looked distant then continued. "No one would choose a lifestyle which brings so much hatred from a society as ignorant as ours."

"I've seen my uncle lose jobs and friends. He even had to move one time because his good neighbors found out and made his life a living hell. They would call at all hours, throw trash all over his lawn and even slashed the tires on his car. After receiving threats against his life he sold his beautiful home at a substantial loss." She hesitated took in a deep breath then looking me straight in the eye answered my question. "Of course I'll keep your secret."

The intensity of her emotion caught me so off guard I had no response.

We finished our coffee in silence before Susan excused herself, saying she had a million things to do.

As she headed for the door, Karen invited her to join us for a picnic.

"When and where?" she smiled.

I looked to Karen who answered, "We don't like to study on an empty stomach so how about in front of the library at about one?"

"I have lots to do but if I can I'll be there." She called back as she walked off toward the campus.

"We'll have plenty so you won't need to bring anything." Karen called as Susan disappeared around the corner.

The library courtyard was full of activity when we arrived just a few minutes before one. We picked an area under some oak trees that provided plenty of shade and started preparing our picnic.

The wind whipped the blanket as we attempted to spread it. It didn't seem to matter where we stood or how we held the blanket for the wind seemed to be coming from every direction. Our attempts to get all four corners weighted down had us laughing uncontrollably. Persistence paid off and we were finally able to sit triumphantly in the middle.

Looking into Karen's vibrant blue eyes I could feel myself getting lost in my desire for her. I stopped laughing for it was nearly impossible for me to hold back my urge to take her in my arms and kiss her right then and there. Watching the boy-girl couples openly embrace frustrated me all the more as I reached out and squeezed Karen's hand. Her eyes met mine she gave me a knowing wink, and we were soon laughing again.

As we waited for Susan we watched some squirrels play chase in the nearby trees. They raced to the top where they seemed to defy gravity as they jumped from limb to limb before disappearing into a cluster of leaves.

It was nearly one thirty and we were about to give up on Susan, when I saw her coming through the library doors. A quick wave as I called her name had her heading our way.

"We were about to send out a search party." I said trying to sound irritated.

"Sorry, I got cornered by Janice and would probably still be there if her boyfriend hadn't shown up."

When she realized I was teasing she giggled and knelt on the blanket with us. "So what's on the menu?"

"Let's see," I reached into the wicker basket and began pulling out the goodies.

"We have some of Karen's delicious chicken salad sandwiches, chips, apples, and your choice of water or soda."

Simultaneously Karen opted for water while Susan asked for a soda, diet if we had one.

"Here's a diet soda for Susan and a bottle of water for Karen and myself. Don't be shy there's plenty if you want seconds." I assured them as I fulfilled their requests.

We were enjoying our meal when the squirrels returned and seemed a bit more interested in what we were doing. We threw a few pieces of bread on the ground between them and us. They quickly picked some up and hurried back to the safety of the trees.

They came back for more and one brave squirrel came up and took a piece from Karen's hand.

I'm not sure which was more frightened, the squirrel thinking he might be grabbed at any moment or Karen who seemed afraid it would suddenly attack and bite the hand that fed it.

The squirrels ran off and we settled back to enjoy the last of our meal, when suddenly Paul appeared out of nowhere and was pulling Susan to her feet. "We need to talk." He demanded as he started dragging her along behind him.

Susan pulled back and stood defiantly in front of him. "All right, we'll talk but I'm not going anywhere with you, so let go."

Paul eased his grip but did not let go as Karen and I stood ready to aide Susan if need be.

"I got the message you left on my answering machine." He growled like someone possessed by an evil demon as he spat out the words. "What do you mean? You won't marry me and you never want to see me again?"

"If you had been home instead of out on the town with that girl Sharon, I could have explained it to you then." She spat back at him drawing the attention of anyone who hadn't already stopped to watch the drama unfolding before us. "I'm tired of being treated like a dog to be kept on a short leash."

Paul's eyes seemed darker than usual. "There's nothing going on between me and Sharon and who says I treat you like a dog? These two?" He said through clenched teeth as he glared in our direction.

"No I said it, but even worse than that I feel it." Susan replied holding back tears she refused to let fall. "I want to be more than Mrs. Paul Riley."

Paul's voice softened and he tried to sound sincere, "Sure baby you can be whatever you want to be. I can change just give me another chance."

Susan seemed about to give in when Paul started pulling at her again. "Let's go someplace private to discuss this." His voice was once again cold and impersonal.

She jerked back hard and this time broke free of his grasp. "You're not the kind who can change." Her voice trembled, "The world must always revolve around you, and if not voluntarily then you'll try to force it. I'm getting out while I still can. I left the message on your machine so you couldn't stop me from saying what I needed to say." She continued quickly, "Your reaction proves I'm right. You don't care what I think or feel as long as you get what you want. Now if you don't mind I was having a pleasant outing with my friends until you showed up."

Paul looked taken aback for just a moment then a smile crossed his lips as he tried a new tactic. "Let me tell you something about your friends here." He taunted. "I've heard they are more than roommates." He paused then said the words loud and clear for all to hear. "They're lovers." He snickered glaring at us again.

Paul' was not prepared for the reaction he got to this revelation and Susan knew it. "I've known" She said triumphantly not letting on it was just this morning when she found out, "They make a wonderful couple don't you think?"

Paul's face paled when he realized she knew. He had lost his control over Susan and his voice raged with the want of revenge. "I can hardly wait to tell everyone you're turning Lezbo. You'll be treated like dirt."

It was as if Susan had prepared for this moment for she did not hesitate before she spoke in a cool even tone. "Go right ahead. I'm sure your friends will love hearing how I turned to a woman," she hesitated, and then guffawed "because you couldn't satisfy me."

"You wouldn't dare say such a thing." His face was red with fury as he spat the words.

"I won't have to," she continued to laugh, "it's just what everyone will think no matter what I or anybody else says. You'll be the one who's the brunt of all the jokes, so just go ahead and tell them. I can hardly wait."

Paul had to face the truth. It was over. Susan had broken free and he was powerless to stop it. He turned put his hands in his pockets and walked away without looking back.

CHAPTER 3

The next few weeks were nearly unbearable. It seemed as if everyone at school had heard about Susan and Paul's confrontation in front of the library. The only thing any of them seem to have heard was Karen and I were lovers and Susan might be a lesbian.

Susan could easily put these accusations to rest for after all she was not a lesbian and everyone would be more than happy to accept this truth. She tried to apologize for making our secret so public. We assured her that it wasn't her fault, after all Paul was the one to point out our relationship was already no secret.

People we had considered cordial acquaintances and even friends started avoiding us as if we had the plague. Whenever we entered a room stares and whispers were inevitably followed with laughter. We found ourselves an open target for snide remarks and cruel jokes.

One day Karen came home in tears because someone she had considered a friend told her she wanted nothing to do with a dyke.

"I don't understand why everyone has to be so mean." She asked between sobs. "We haven't done anything to them."

I pulled Karen into my arms held her close and rocked her back and forth. I wanted to shield her from an unkind world. "There are a lot of people who are afraid of what they don't understand. If she had been a true friend she would have gotten past your life style."

Wiping the tears from her eyes I suggested. "It might be easier if we deny the rumors. They are all so homophobic. They would be relieved to hear it was all just a joke on Paul."

Karen reflected a moment then replied. "It might work for awhile but sooner or later someone will notice an innocent yet intimate touch or a soul searching glance from across a crowded room. It will be impossible to hide our love for long."

She was right; it would be nearly impossible to hide our love under such close scrutiny. I didn't want to cheapen my love for Karen with such a lie just to calm the fears of the people around us; however we would have to do something before the school got involved.

As mid-term exams neared everyone was to busy studying to worry about the lesbians and how horrible it was they were going to this school.

It was Friday and waiting for test results was proving to be just as nerve racking as preparing for them had been. Karen and I were getting ready for a much-needed night out when the phone rang. A very lonely sounding Susan was on the other end. "So what are you guys doing tonight?"

When I told her a night of drinking and dancing, she explained how Paul's friends had made it next to impossible for her to enjoy an evening out.

"Can I tag along with you and Karen?" She asked.

I tried to explain. "A well it's a women's bar and you might . . ."

"I won't mind." She jumped in before I could get out any more objections.

"I don't have anything against women being together."

I took a deep breath and continued with the only real objection I could find.

"Some of the women will resent some straight person coming in just to gawk at them."

Susan was determined to go and countered. I don't want to gawk. I just want to go out and have some fun. Come on Pleaaase, besides they don't have to know I'm straight. I wont tell, if you don't"

My resistance was waning as I asked. "What will you do when someone asks you to dance?"

"If they do I'll just say no thank you." She insisted then giggled and added mischievously, "Unless of course I want to dance."

"Right," I hesitated then reluctantly gave in. "OK you win we'll pick you up in an hour."

The excitement was clear in her voice as she assured me she would be ready and waiting that I almost laughed out loud. However the expression on Karen's face as I hung up the phone assured me of something else, I had lost my mind.

It was getting late by the time we got to the club. Many familiar faces greeted us as we made our way to a table being cleared near the dance floor. I noticed a lot of them checking out Susan.

I couldn't wait to tell Susan how this is where Karen and I had met. She listened intently as I told her the story. "Luckily the drinking age was not changing to 21 for a few months or we might never have met. "I had just got my acceptance letter from the college and decided to celebrate by checking out the local color. I was sitting over there." I said as I pointed toward a table near the bar. "Karen was sitting with a group of friends at the table next to mine."

My eyes kept drifting in her direction, then would quickly dart anywhere else when she would glance my way. It was almost hypnotic the way her laughter flowed, easy not forced or held back, while her eyes were filled with delight.

Even though all were turned down I was filled with envy, as I watched several others ask her to dance. I thought of how it would be worth it just for the chance to be close to her for the moment it took to ask. I noticed every now and then she would look my way. I was sure it was only my overactive and very hopeful imagination. What's the worst that could happen? She would say no, right? I would go quietly back to my table have another beer and then go home."

"Sounds like you had it bad." Susan laughed.

"Yeah, it was love at first sight for me and if being turned down had been my only fear it would have been easy. My real fear was that she would say yes. Oh, I could move with the music or tap my foot to the beat as long as I was safe in my seat but on the dance floor I became like an arthritic old woman afraid to move for fear of the pain it would cause."

In an attempt to bolster my courage I flagged down the waitress and ordered another drink. When I turned to look in Karen's direction again all I found there was an empty chair.

My heart sank to realize I had missed my chance to meet this woman who had so enchanted me. I frantically scanned the room in hopes of at least a final glimpse of her before she disappeared into the night possibly lost to me forever.

I started with the outer room where it was least crowded then slowly narrowed my search to the dance floor. I was scanning the sea of dancers when I felt a tap on my shoulder as an unfamiliar voice asked if I was looking for someone.

When I turned to see it was Karen I nearly choked on the simple words . . . "No, not really."

"Well then would you like to dance?" she asked.

I could not believe my ears or my eyes and was so dumbfounded I couldn't reply.

Karen hesitated then said. "I would have waited for you to ask but it is getting late."

Still having trouble getting words to come out I swallowed and was able to get out one word . . . "Sure."

"Um why don't you leave your hat at the table?"

I thought this was an odd request then as if reading my thoughts she added, "I don't think you have to worry about anyone stealing it."

I laid the hat on the table and she said," I nodded toward Karen who was listening as intently as Susan but being strangely quite. "Good now I can see your eyes." to which I smiled.

As if by magic a slow song started just as we reached the dance floor. We swayed to the music holding each other close. The touch of her skin was silky smooth on mine and the sweet aroma of her perfume drew me closer. I was certain I would soon awaken from what must be a dream and have to take a cold shower.

When we got back to the table my hat was gone. Karen was so apologetic all I could do was laugh. Karen admitted to having requested the slow song and I admitted she had been the object of my frantic search. We dated for a couple of months before deciding to share an apartment and we've been together ever since.

Karen smiled mischievously as she asked. "Now would you like to hear my version of what happened that night?"

Susan was wide eyed, looking like a child who had just been offered the last piece of cake when she said, "Yes"

Karen's eyes met mine and held for a moment before she asked. "Are you sure you want to hear this?" This question was directed to me.

This stirred my curiosity as well for we had never talked about the night we met. With full confidence of a positive reflection, I smiled, "Of course I want to hear it."

She hesitated, smiled, and then started "Well as Lynn said I was sitting over there with a group of my friends. Lynn drew everyone's attention when she entered the bar, and not just because she was new." Maybe I didn't want to hear this after all. "She was wearing a pair of black slacks, a white shirt, and a heavy dark jacket for which it was much to warm."

"Hey I was dressed to meet women. What's a little discomfort besides it's what I feel comfortable in." I stretched out my arms indicating I was dressed much the same way to night.

Karen laughed at my unease and continued. "Her hair was tied in a pony tail behind her head, and she was wearing a really awful hat."

"Hey it was a great hat. It went with the outfit." I defended quickly.

"Yes Hon it did go with the outfit but it hid most of your face. Anyway a couple of us whispered the same thought simultaneously. ""Oh no lesbian Mafia."" We were all laughing so hard." I could feel my body tensing up.

Susan stifled a laugh when she noticed how uncomfortable I was getting.

"With tears in our eyes we watched Lynn walk across the room so confident and unaware she was the object of our bemusement. We stifled our laughter as she took a seat at a table near by. We were then laughing because we could not stop laughing." Karen and Susan were both smiling at me as she went on. Nope I did not like this version one little bit I thought as my cheeks burned bright red with embarrassment.

Karen leaned over and kissed my cheek before continuing. "Honestly we were all checking her out, after all that is what everyone does when a new woman comes into the bar." I smiled uneasily for this made me feel a little better but after what I'd heard so far I was still wary of what was yet to come.

Karen smiled as she continued. "It was hard to tell because the hat hid her eyes and she would turn her head if I even happened to look her way, but she was watching our table."

"At one point I watched as she peeled the label slowly from her beer bottle and put the pieces in a neat little pile at the center of the table. I had always thought this an irritating habit because it would leave a mess for someone else to clean up later. I couldn't help but smile as she picked up each little piece and neatly." Susan interrupted and finished the thought. "Put it into the empty bottle." It was as if they were sharing a personal secret. "I've seen her do it hundreds of times."

My tension was mounting. "I only do that when I'm bored or as in this case nervous as hell."

"Although I love to dance I turned down all offers, not because of miss thing here but because I was cramping so bad. Feeling bloated and entirely unattractive, I was not up to meeting anyone that night."

At this I winced. "No more, please." I begged.

"It only gets better from here, I promise." Karen took my hand in hers and squeezed.

"Oh all right go ahead rip my heart out the rest of the way." I smiled, trying to hide the truth I felt in my words.

"Our waitress had disappeared and we were ready for another round so I went to the bar to place our order. From the other end of the bar I saw Lynn look toward my table then start searching the room. As I watched her I had the sudden feeling I had to meet her.

After placing my order I made my way to the DJ's booth. I tipped her a dollar to play a nice slow song but to give me a few minutes before she started it."

"I was so nervous I stood behind you for a long time trying to think of something witty to say. My friends were looking at me as if they thought I had lost my mind. I knew the current song was about to end and the one I had requested would soon start. It was now or never so I decided to ask what I really wanted to know.

When I asked if she were looking for someone and our eyes met for the very first time, it felt magical, as if our souls touched." As she continued I thought back to that moment and was filled with the same intense feelings I had experienced at the time. "Such pretty eyes so warm and inviting they drew me right in. I thought it a shame to hide them behind her hat and knew it had to go. When we got to the dance floor you hesitated."

"That's because I can't dance. I just knew I would step all over your feet dancing to a slow song."

"I thought you had changed your mind and were about to go back to your table so I took your hand in mine. My fingers tingled at the touch and I felt you tremble as I guided your arm around me. You held me close and it felt right. I was afraid you had not felt the connection and wanted the song to go on indefinitely. I was relieved when you asked me back to your table. I nearly choked trying to hold back my laughter when you realized your hat was gone. I felt bad your hat had disappeared but was secretly glad it was gone."

"I never told you because I was afraid you would think our dance had been some sort of plot. I found out later that my friends had taken your hat."

Susan was halfway through her second Long Island Ice Tea by the time Karen finished her version of the night.

"I think I like Karen's version better." Susan said, her words slightly slurred.

I pulled Karen onto my lap wrapped my arms lovingly around her and agreed. "I do to." Then I kissed her gently "and you had better slow down, those drinks are potent."

Susan smiled "Don't worry two's my limit then it's virgins after that." This made us all laugh.

Playing chaperone was making me more nervous than Susan, who to my surprise accepted a few requests for a dance. On her third trip to the dance floor I couldn't help but laugh as a slow song started and she politely asked to sit this one out promising the next upbeat one.

It was a pleasant evening and Susan had made several new friends. When I teased her at having broken a few hearts she assured me all knew she was unavailable.

We went to a nearby café that was a popular after hours stop. As usual it was full of drunks trying to sober up before heading home.

The cringe on Susan's face as she looked around the room made me take a closer look at the place myself. The plain white wallpaper had long ago yellowed from the smoke that always hung heavy in the air. The vinyl seat covers were cracked and dry, while the floor though clean was in need of some major repair. It was definitely not the ambiance bringing us to this place.

I quickly suggested we go elsewhere but Susan insisted it was OK and this would be just fine. Once we had been seated a pimply-faced young man served us coffee. Susan finally asked, "Why do you come here?"

There was only one reason I could give as I explained, "It's one of the few places we can go and actually sit together holding hands without feeling like criminals."

"I see." She almost whispered as a spark of understanding glistened in her eyes accompanied by a gentle smile.

Although it was nearly 2:30am when we dropped Susan off, we decided to go for a drive. We ended up in Galveston where we went for a moonlit walk along the deserted beach.

The moon was bright enough we could look for seashells as we walked barefoot along the shoreline. The waves washed over our feet as tiny particles of sand tickled through our toes. We turned to go just as the sun began to peek over the horizon.

Karen suddenly knelt down and I thought she had cut herself on a piece of glass or something. As I knelt down beside her she scooped something from the water. She laughed like a child as she stared at the starfish as it wiggled in the palm of her hand. I watched amazed at this woman-child before me as I found a new depth in my love for her.

She let the starfish slip gently back into the water before turning to face me.

Still on our knees our eyes met, locked, filling me with an uncontrollable urge to take her in my arms and make love to her right there on the beach. When I leaned forward to kiss her she pulled away.

Still flush with desire I came to my senses and quickly kissed her on the cheek.

I helped her up and we found a secluded spot where we could sit together undisturbed. I sat behind Karen and held her in my arms as we watched sailboats silhouetted by the orange glow of the sunrise making their way out into the bay.

We spent the rest of the morning and most of the afternoon sleeping then went to dinner with Frank and Carl at a restaurant full of fellow students. Carl took me by surprise when he got down on one knee and handed me a ring box. I looked at him puzzled.

Smiling he whispered so only I could hear. "This is as close to getting married as I ever want to get." I smiled back as I opened the box and found a friendship ring inside. It looked enough like an engagement ring that others would assume it was.

"Friends forever." I whispered back to him before giving him a kiss to complete the performance. This show of affection quelled most of the rumors but we could still feel many eyes upon us whenever we were together.

$\mathcal{C}$HAPTER 4

It was a relief to find out Karen had done well on all her exams, for anything below a B would send her into a blue funk for weeks. The result of overbearing parents who always insisted she make straight A's; however by high school they had reluctantly gave in and some B's would be acceptable.

Though I had studied extensively my results indicated I needed improvement, especially in History and English. At lunch Susan insisted she needed to talk and asked if I could stop by her place after school. Knowing Karen would be working, I accepted the invitation. As I knocked on the door I wondered what she wanted to talk about.

Susan opened the door slowly and seemed very nervous. She was wearing black slacks and silk blouse. The blouse was a shade of turquoise that brought out the deep blue of her eyes and fit to accentuate her ample breasts. I figured she had a date and this would not take long.

I accepted her offer of a drink and made myself comfortable on the sofa. She put on some music and lay on the love seat across from me as though she were posing for some magazine layout.

Susan was so nervous that I didn't rush her even though I had many things to do. We sat in silence sipping our drinks until I could wait no longer. I had to break the silence. "What's with the music?"

"I thought you liked Barbara." She replied as she shifted to a sitting position on the edge of the love seat.

"I do but I've never known you to be a big fan. I didn't even know you owned one of her albums."

"I was playing it to relax you."

"Relax me?" I questioned. "You're the one who needs to relax. Now come on what's up?"

"Well I have a personal question to ask and don't quite know how to bring it up." She said coyly.

"Now is your chance, ask away." I sat on the edge of my seat more curious than ever.

"I was wondering," she hesitated then taking a deep breath continued "do you and Karen go out with other people?"

Unable to figure out this line of questioning, I answered as honestly as I could. "Well we never really discussed it but as far as I know the answer is no." As I spoke the words I felt something awful churning in the pit of my stomach. The worst possible scenario flashed through my mind, Karen was seeing someone else and somehow Susan had found out and was about to tell me all about it.

Panic was about to take over when another possibility crossed my mind. This one was as hard to believe and as unlikely as the first had been. "Susan," I could feel the color rising in my cheeks as I asked. "Are you making a pass at me?" I could not hide the smile spreading over my face.

"No," her voice quivered as she turned so I could not see her eyes "of course not." Then she stood up and looked me straight in the eye. "What if I am? Is that such a repulsive a thought?"

It was hard not to laugh but sensing a deeper pain I went and put my arms around her. "No, not at all, I'm flattered. Since I met Karen I haven't considered anyone else in that way. Besides I've always thought of us as sisters and you, you caught me totally off guard."

Trying to find the right words I continued, "Sometimes there's a fine line between friends and lovers and most people who cross the line are sorry they did. The friendship doesn't usually survive once the passion is gone."

"Then you admit there is an attraction?" she asked trying to meet my eyes again.

I simply avoided the question and her eyes by continuing. "You've always talked about getting married and having kids. I know you're lonely and are probably curious but I believe you still want those same things now."

"And if I don't?" she asked seductively.

I felt as if I were trying to dodge a bullet that was following my every move.

"Think about it for awhile then if you still want to date a woman I can introduce you to some who are available." I smiled warmly, releasing her from my arms. She seemed so lost and alone. I immediately wanted to hold her again but resisted the temptation.

"Can I ask another question?" She spoke quickly.

"Sure," I said uncertain how I would answer any more questions of this type.

"When did you know you preferred women to men?" she asked getting up to fix us another drink.

"I'm not really sure when it started but I can tell you my first clear memory."

She handed me a drink then sat on a chair so that we were facing one another. Things felt more normal and I was able to relax I started my story.

"It was the summer I turned thirteen. A friend and I had gone to play in the park. Cindy was her name, tall, skinny, a natural blond with deep blue eyes."

"Like mine?" Susan interrupted.

I looked at her, took a calming breath, "Yes" then immediately continued my story. "We were at the park where I lay down on the grass and closed my eyes. 'What are you doing?' She asked.

'Getting in touch with mother earth.' I said quite sure of myself. 'I have this theory how in walking upright we lose some vital link.' She stared at me as if I had gone mad so I added, 'It may look silly but it does make me feel better. Come on and give it a try.' I motioned for her to lie beside me.

After close inspection to make sure there were no bugs she lay next to me and closed her eyes. 'Now clear your mind of everything and breathe deeply.' I instructed.

I found the aroma of her perfume very distracting and before long communing with Mother Nature was not what I had in mind. I watched as she lay there with her eyes closed. Her hair lay on the ground circling her sweet face like a golden halo, while steady even breaths raised and lowered her budding breasts. I don't know where it came from or why I felt it at all but I had a strong desire to just reach out and touch them. My heat raced at the thought of just reaching out and brushing a finger over them. I daydreamed of my secret desires, aching for them to become a reality.

I was reaching out to touch one when her eyes opened and she sat up quickly.

Thanks to some quick thinking, I pretended to brush a bug from her shoulder. Horrified some creepy crawly thing had been on her, she suggested we play something else.

I was so confused, I couldn't figure out why I felt this way. While all of the other girls were going boy crazy, I had no interest in them at all.

I wanted to like boys and I wanted them to like me. In my attempts to hide or overcome my secret desires I became very popular. I would go on dates with any boy who would ask, and soon got the undeserved reputation of being easy. One date became the general rule, as they were shocked to find I was a virgin and intent on staying one.

I dated one guy for awhile but he found another girl because I would not help him save my reputation with the truth. Looking back I feel guilty for using him as a cover when he truly cared for me. How could I possibly tell him that I needed the lies to hide my secret, how like most boys at Sheldon High, I was pining away over the cheer leading squad?

My senior year I didn't bother to date at all. Rumors flew . . . It was said I had been pregnant and lost the baby or perhaps I had given it up for adoption. It was also rumored I'd had a religious experience and changed my ways. The fact I was a lesbian tired of dating boys with only one thing on their mind was never even hinted at.

I should have known I was a lesbian sooner, but what was to know? I never dreamed others felt the same and had never heard words to describe how I was feeling. When I did hear words like Homo or gay it was in quiet whispers and very clearly taboo.

Mid-term you transferred to our school and we became friends but I couldn't tell you my secret. I couldn't tell anyone. When I found others who felt the same it was such a relief. It was clear I had always been a lesbian."

As I finished the story Susan offered me another drink but I excused myself, "I really must be going. I have a ton of things to do before Karen gets home."

"It's all right," she assured me "I've got some serious thinking to do and need some time alone."

As she closed the door behind me I felt relieved to be out of there. I was worried about leaving her alone but did not want to confuse her anymore than I already had.

I didn't see Susan for several weeks and was not really surprised when I ran into her at the bar. I was however surprised to find that she was there with a date. A tall woman with dark hair and equally dark eyes stood as Susan introduced us.

This woman who was about five or six years older than Susan unnerved me, not because of her age but because of her appearance. The faded blue jeans, leather jacket and the extremely short haircut gave her the appearance of what I had considered a dyke.

Susan introduced her as Kim who seemed unsure of how to greet us as she reached out a shaky hand in our direction. I smiled as best I could and gave her a firm handshake. "Nice to meet you," we said in unison which would usually bring laughter at a time like this but I was too wary to be humorous.

Karen sensing the tension between us insisted Susan join her in the ladies room. The long lines would assure us plenty of time to talk. We started as soon as they were out of hearing range.

"So Lynn do you know Susan is in love with you?" Kim asked almost accusingly.

"No she is not" I insisted "She just envies what I have with Karen and thinks because she hasn't found it with a man that maybe she will be able to find it with a woman. I'm afraid when she comes to her senses you'll both get hurt."

"You could be wrong." She said hopefully.

It was obvious she really cared for Susan so I relaxed a little. "I admit I could be wrong. You and Susan may live happily ever after, if there is such a thing. I'm just asking you to take it slow and not rush her into something she's not ready for."

"You don't have to worry about it. I really like Susan and know if I rush her I'll only scare her off and I don't want that." she tried to assure me.

Seeing Karen and Susan making their way back to us, I added as authoritatively as I could, "One more thing if you ever do anything to hurt Susan you'll have to answer to me."

She didn't have time to reply but our eyes met for an instant and I knew she understood my warning.

"You two seem to be getting along quite well." Susan smiled as if she excited she had been the subject of our discussion. "Whatever were you talking about?"

"Actually we were talking about you." Kim smiled mischievously and winked at Susan. "All of it good, you're lucky to have such a good friend." She added looking in my direction.

"Yes I know." Susan put her hand on mine and gave it a squeeze before turning her full attention to Kim.

I tried not to watch over them but continually found myself looking their way. Karen seemed relieved when I suggested we leave. It was still early and the café was nearly empty when we arrived.

We sat across from each other as usual and ordered coffee. Karen sat in silence for awhile then with tears in her eyes asked, "Are you in love with Susan?"

I started to laugh but saw the pain she was feeling. I moved to her side putting my arm around her. Near tears myself, "No baby I love you and only you. I'm sorry I spent so much time worrying about her tonight." I gently wiped urs as I explained. "Susan's a friend who is headed to fast and for all the wrong reasons."

"Why should it concern you?" Karen demanded.

"She's a friend, but I also feel we inadvertently sent her in the direction she's headed. She wants what we have," I smiled and pulled her closer, "and I feel responsible for anything that might happen to her."

"Are you sure there is not more to it?" She sniffled.

"Yes," I said holding her face in my hands looking into her eyes. The uncertainty I saw there was breaking my heart and I feared that no words would ever be enough to remove those doubts.

I leaned forward and kissed her in hopes she would feel the love filling my heart. When I pulled back our eyes met and locked in the old familiar way. I smiled and she smiled back. We went home to explore the uniqueness of our love and I would be very careful not to give her any reason to doubt my love again.

Susan did not like talking about Kim and when I would ask how things were going she would just say fine and refuse any further comment. One day when I asked she would not respond at all. When I tried to make eye contact she would not allow it.

"Susan," I practically shouted to get her attention. "What's wrong?" She would not answer so I asked. "Has Kim done something to you?" The tension was thick in my voice.

"No she has not done anything to me and I do not want to talk about it." She would not let her eyes meet mine.

I tried to get her to talk but she would not. Once she left I realized the only way to get answers would be to talk to Kim. I knew Susan would not tell me where she lived so my search would have to begin at the bar.

The bartenders knew most of the regulars and remembered Kim. "She plays pool and will be here for the tournament Thursday night."

I thanked the bartender and could hardly wait for Thursday. When I arrived the tournament had already started and it was Kim's turn to play.

"We'll talk after the game." She said gruffly.

I watched as the balls disappeared one by one as the girls took their turns. Kim was an excellent player calling her shots and making most of them seem effortless while the other girl took lots of time to aim each shot. Finally only the eight ball remained and it was Kim's turn.

She held her stick carefully. "Corner pocket." She called nodding her head to indicate which corner.

From what I could see of the angles, I was sure she would miss. She pulled back the stick slow and steady, then gave it a sudden thrust forward to meet the cue ball. The cue ball hit the eight with great force then stopped where the impact had occurred while the eight bounced off the side and rolled with a slight curve to the left.

To my amazement it was headed straight toward the designated pocket when stopped so close to the edge that I'm sure if anyone had breathed it would have fallen in.

Her opponent made the easy shot to the cheers of her friends at having beaten the more experienced player. Kim congratulated the winner who was all smiles and then headed my direction.

"To bad," I greeted her "I thought you were going to make it."

She looked confused for a moment then smiled. "Oh the shot. I have to let them win once in awhile or they won't play me. I don't usually give in so early though."

"I thought this was a tournament?"

"It is but the prize is only a fifty dollar bar tab. You should see me play when the prize is serious money," she said smiling as she led me to an empty table at the far end of the bar. "Is this OK or would you prefer to go somewhere more private?"

I looked around the room and saw most watching the tournament and the rest were lovers absorbed in each other. "This will be fine." I waited till we were seated then asked, "You know why I'm here?"

"Not really." She was looking past me to the on going game, "but I figure it has something to do with Susan."

"I told you how you would have to answer to me if you ever did anything to hurt Susan."

"I remember, so why are you here?" she asked without taking her eyes off the tournament.

"I've come to find out what you did to her?" I said accusingly in hopes of getting her full attention.

It worked, her eyes narrowed as she looked at me. "What exactly did she tell you?"

"Nothing," I admitted and then angrily added. "Which means it must have been really bad."

"I am not as rough around the edges as I may look. I would never take advantage of or do anything to hurt Susan." She said unconcerned of my apparent anger.

"Damn it. I know something happened so just tell me what it was?" I leaned across the table nearly nose to nose with her. I knew I would probably end up with a black eye if I kept pushing but I had to know.

She held eye contact with me for a few moments. "Susan should be the one telling you this but I can see how you are only concerned for her well being."

"That's right . . ." I started but she held up her hand to silence me.

"You're not fooling anyone with this tough act so just sit down and listen." She stared off into the distance as if looking into the past closed her eyes and took a deep breath as I sat back into my seat. "Before I begin I want you to know Susan is the kind of woman I would like to spend the rest of my life with."

She smiled a tight smile then continued. "We were at her place watching a movie on cable. We had been drinking and were very relaxed. I slipped my arm around her at which she leaned closer. I leaned over and we kissed. Our very first kiss." She smiled "Delicately our lips brushed together; gently I parted her lips with my tongue. I could feel the hunger of her passion, which seemed to rage as much as my own. Our tongues intertwined and my entire body was flooded with desire. It was wonderful." Kim was breathing heavily.

"O.K. that's enough, I don't want to hear anymore. I started to get up and leave.

"No wait, you wanted to know. So sit back down, your gonna hear it all." She leaned to blocked my path. All I could do was sit back down and gaze at the table wanting to hear but not really wanting to know what was coming next.

"Susan reached out her hand which brushed lightly against my breast. I was on fire as shivers of passion coursed through my body." She paused as if it were unbearable to remember let alone speak. Painfully she continued, "Susan suddenly froze and pulled away. She said we had to stop that it was all a mistake she had momentarily forgotten she was with a woman and she couldn't allow it to go any further.

Then she started babbling about how her parents would never understand and how it was a sin, but of course we could still be friends. Needless to say the evening quickly fizzled and I went home to a cold shower." She hesitated reflectively then added "I don't think it will be long before she's dating men again."

I felt sorry for her and the pain she was going through, but not knowing what to do or say I merely thanked her for telling me something Susan never would and left.

CHAPTER 5

There would be no easy way to approach Susan with what I had learned from Kim so I decided to wait for her to bring up the subject. Unfortunately would not be until six months later on her wedding day. She had asked me to be her maid of honor and though I didn't like wearing a dress I consented to for this special occasion.

Susan's father was looking at his watch about every minute or so as he paced back and forth. He was making Susan even more nervous so she insisted, "Dad I need to talk with Marilynn," I was surprised by her use of my seldom used given name.

Without a word he moved over and stood by the door. "Alone dad" she insisted. He reluctantly left the room. It was as if he thought I'd run off with the bride in some weird version of The Graduate.

Once the door closed and we were sure he was not listening at the door. I was able to ask the question I had been trying to ask since the day she told me of her sudden decision to get married to a man I hadn't even met. "Why are you in such a hurry to get married? When she would not answer I asked, "Maybe this is what you think your parents want or are you're trying to save yourself from your true feelings?" When she wouldn't answer I tried another question. "What I really want to know is do you love him?"

"You've talked to Kim haven't you?" She asked effectively changing the subject.

"Yes, I know I shouldn't have but I did and she told me all about the night of your first kiss and it's nothing to be embarrassed about. I don't know why you couldn't be the one to tell me."

"I could never have gone through with it if we hadn't drunk ourselves silly." Susan said nonchalantly as she looked in the mirror fixing her vale.

"Gone through with what?" I put my hand on a chair to steady myself aware I was not as informed as I had thought.

"Why sleeping with Kim of course." Then realizing the extent of her revelation giggled, "I guess she didn't tell you everything."

"That liar, to think I was actually feeling sorry for her when she told me what happened." Only slightly shocked at what I was hearing now.

"Tell me what she said and I'll let you know how much of it is true." Susan teased.

I related Kim's story at which Susan closed her eyes and smiled at the memory. "All true except for the pulling back part. She had no need of a cold shower that night as we showered together quite warm and cozy."

"So why did you stop seeing her?" It didn't make sense and I wanted to know.

"It was a couple of weeks before I realized how I still wanted to be a wife and mother, not having to hide my love like some dirty little secret." she said the words as if they left a bad taste in her mouth. I winced at the truth in her words. "I'm sorry Lynn; I didn't mean to cause you any pain."

"Society put the dagger of guilt there. You just twisted it enough to remind me of its existence." I assured her before getting back to the only question which really mattered, "Sooo . . . . Why are you in such a hurry to get married?"

She relaxed and actually hugged herself before answering. "It's simple. I love Roger more than I thought I could ever love anyone. I don't want to give him the chance to change his mind." she said with a glowing smile.

I gave her a quick hug and a light kiss on the cheek. "That's all I wanted to know and it is the only reason anyone should ever get married." I smiled back at her. "Any time your ready Miss soon to be Mrs."

"Not quite yet," she had a mischievous look in her eye as she stopped me from opening the door. "You know it's tradition for everyone to kiss the bride on her wedding day. To save my parents the embarrassment I want to collect one from you now." she insisted then specified" and I want a real kiss."

"You know you don't have to get married just to get a kiss from me." I smiled as I took her in my arms then brought my lips close to hers. I held back for a moment then lightly touched my lips to hers. I was surprised by the sudden desire filling me, a desire that brought us much closer than friends but not quite to the point of lovers. As our lips parted Susan took my lower lip gently between her teeth as if not wanting it to end.

"If only that were true." She said sadly.

I looked into her deep blue eyes and said, "I want you to know I think you're beautiful and I'll always be your friend."

"Yeah, yeah, I know." She sighed before we signaled them to start the music.

Her father seemed relieved as we opened the door and took our places for the ceremony to begin.

As they spoke their words of love my attention was drawn to the third row on the bride's side where Karen sat. She was smiling back at me and I knew she was the only one I wanted to spend my life with.

With the ceremony over and the reception a success, we wished the bride and groom well amid a shower of rice. They paused at the door just long enough for Susan to throw the bouquet. It was deliberately coming straight at me when a group of girls scrambled in front of me. The victor was a lanky young cousin of Susan's. They gave a quick smile and wave, before climbing into their tin can laden, Chevy.

Later at home we lay on the sofa in such a way that Karen was in front of me her head back to resting just below mine. "Karen," I whispered. She turned her head just enough to let me know she was listening. My voice faltered slightly "If we could would you marry me?"

She didn't say anything for a long time then asked, "Why would you want to go through all that? It's such a headache. Besides you know they won't let us. It's not legal." I was glad she could not see my eyes as my heart sank.

Karen seemed certain this could never be a possibility and maybe she was right. Why worry about something you can never have. I held her close and tried not to think about how my entire being still longed to hear her say yes.

CHAPTER 6

Karen had the flyer for the Desert Hearts Cowgirl ranch of Bandera Texas in her hand as she tried to make reservations.

"How far in advance?" She asked unhappily. "I know it's a lot to ask but we where hoping you would have something available this weekend," she kicked her foot against the desk "anything will do." She added trying to sound hopeful but not succeeding.

She moved the phone from her mouth, so as not to shout in the woman's ear. "We're in luck." She gave me the thumbs up and I think would have done a summersault if she wasn't afraid of loosing the connection.

She wrote down a lot of directions then got busy packing.

Frank was visiting his parents and had loaned us his convertible for the long drive. It made us feel alive to have the wind whip through our hair as made the trek west from Houston to San Antonio along Interstate 10.

Excited by the much needed get away from everything weekend we howled as we pulled up to the gate. Karen jumped out of the car before I could even get it in park. She opened the gate then closed it behind the car before getting back in. We maneuvered the rocky drive through cedar trees that made it impossible to see any other part of the ranch. About halfway down the drive we found an empty coral so continued on to the end of the drive where we parked in the shade next to a pick-up already parked there.

We followed the walkway to a small stone building where we found a welcome sign on the door. There was also the letter D followed by the shape of a heart branded on the door to assure us we were at the right place.

We knocked on the door but there was no answer. When we tried the knob it turned so we opened the door and called out. "Hello, anybody home?" We entered slowly and took a quick look around. We thought it best to wait outside when we found the place empty. We were going to look around for someone, however not knowing where to start we decided it best to wait near the cottage.

We sat on a swing bench next to a fire pit to the right of the cottage. There were other chairs but the bench was cozy enough for two. We looked out over a breath taking view that was not the sagebrush and desert I had expected for west Texas. We saw trees on hills with a creek running through that was so beautiful I vowed to explore as much of it as I could during our stay.

The owners came walking down the trail followed by a dog and were surprised to find we had made it down the driveway unnoticed.

"Hi, I see you found us." She welcomed us warmly.

"Your directions were perfect, right down to the wagon wheel on the gate." I assured her.

"I'm Lean this is Bonz and our four legged friend is Mariah."

"I'm Lynn and this is Karen." I said putting my arm around Karen.

We followed them back to the cottage where we had done a quick search earlier. On closer inspection we found there were two bedrooms with a shared kitchen and bath.

They led us into the kitchen where the hollow tone of each step on the wood floor filled me with warmth I could not explain.

We sat at the kitchen table where Lean explained the rules and dangers of the area. She then gave us release forms to sign before we would be allowed to explore the ranch. Dinner was provided with the room so Lean and Bonz started preparing it while Karen and I went off to explore.

We went down some stone steps to the bottom of the hill where a pool was set up. It was a simple above ground pool that would be sufficient for cooling off on a hot Texas afternoon. Further down we found the water trough for the horses and noticed four gold fish swimming happily. We wondered why they where there and would have to ask later.

The sound of running water drew us to a nearby creek. We were delighted to find another bench swing where we sat and watched the water cascade over a rocky edge then plummet into a clear pool below. Such a pleasant spot we hated to leave but dinner would be ready soon and we didn't want to keep our hosts waiting.

They had prepared a tasty Cowgirl chili over tortilla chips. This was the first time I had seen hominy in chili and I was reluctant to try it but I must admit that despite my reservations it was quite tasty.

During dinner we learned the gold fish helped keep the water clean by eating the oats that washed off the horses mouths as they drank. The mention of horses reminded us to make arrangements for a ride in the morning.

Having eaten our fill we declined the chocolate cake was offered for desert. We offered to help with the dishes but Lean and Bonz would not hear of it. When they finished in the kitchen they bid us good night and were off to a party with friends. Other guests would be arriving in the morning but for now we had the entire place to ourselves.

Afraid of getting lost in the dark we stayed near the cottage. Mariah the dog came by to check on us occasionally as if it were her job to do so. We sat on the bench swing and watched humming birds flutter from flower to flower so quickly it was hard to keep track of where they were at any given moment.

"Let's go swimming." Karen suggested with a smile.

"All right let's go." We went inside and closed the blue curtains with the cowgirls on them. They had been drawn back so we could enjoy the view. We changed quickly as Karen put on her blue two-piece while I being more self-conscious wore a black one piece.

The sun was beginning to hang low in the sky as we lit the tiki torches lined the steps we descended to the pool.

Having always been intrigued by the thought of skinny dipping I was tempted to do it now as I teasingly lowered one strap and then the other. I knew the place was deserted and Karen was more than willing to give it a try but I could not quite bring myself to do it.

We splashed around a bit then slowly worked ourselves to a fever of desire as we fondled one another to the edge of ecstasy. We abandoned the pool, making our way up the stone steps by the glow of the tiki torches. As we stopped at each one to put out the flame a passionate kiss and embrace kept our inner fires burning.

With the last torch out we were ready to head for the cottage but had to stop. Awed by the brilliance of the night sky we looked heavenward. Never had I seen the stars so clearly and we vowed find time for some star gazing while we were here.

Karen tugged at my hand reminding me we had other needs to fulfill then turned and ran toward the cottage. She managed to stay ahead of me but had trouble getting the door open. I caught her there, spun her around and pinned her to it. I held her for a moment gazing at her like some lovesick teenager then kissed her as I reached behind her and opened the door. Karen laughed as we tripped over the threshold and fell to the floor.

We helped each other up and took the room to the left of the entrance. The other room had a fireplace but it was much to hot to enjoy, so we decided on the larger room.

I was eager to have Karen out of her wet suit as I pulled the straps from her shoulders. I teased her erect nipples with my tongue as I reached around to undo the final snap.

I quickly slipped off my own suit and was enjoying our reflections in the mirror when Karen turned off the light.

"Hey that's not fair." I cried out but had no trouble finding her in the dark. We became one in the night and made love until exhausted we fell asleep in one another's arms.

We were sleeping peacefully when the phone rang. Lean was calling to make sure hadn't changed our minds about going for a ride.

"No. We're running a little late but are really looking forward to the ride." I assured her.

"There's no rush," Lean replied, "after all this is your vacation and you should be allowed to sleep in if you want."

"We'll be ready in about an hour." I said before hanging up the phone. I gently kissed Karen who had gone back to sleep while I was on the phone. She kissed me back then pulled me closer and began to explore my body with her hands.

"We don't have time for this." I moaned in pleasure as well as regret. "I told them we would be ready in an hour." Karen looked at me blankly needing more information to go on.

"Trail ride." I reminded her. "You get in the shower and I'll see what's in the kitchen." Karen obediently headed for the shower while I went to the kitchen and turned on the coffee pot, which Lean had so thoughtfully prepared the night before. I put cereal bowls and spoons on the table then got out Karen's favorite cereal, Lucky Charms, which we had brought with us.

Having both showered we were half dressed and rushing to get ready when a click at the door sent us racing for the bedroom. We had forgotten that this was a shared area and as we closed the door behind us we heard Lean's voice. "Are you finding everything you need?"

"Yes," we giggled. "We'll be out soon."

When we emerged from the room Bonz had arrived and joined us for breakfast. "We'll have the horses ready in about half and hour." Lean said after cleaning the kitchen. I felt uncomfortable having them clean up after us but was quickly reminded we were the guests when I offered to help.

Karen and I waited on the bench outside. We watched a group of hawks soar high in the early morning sky. They seemed to be racing the clouds which were gently rolling in. I wondered what it must be like to fly so high and free.

I'm sure it was just my imagination but when I put my arm around Karen, I felt as if, we had been touched by some unseen force that strengthened the bond between us.

We headed for the corral where Lean and Bonz were almost finished saddling the horses. We watched as they tightened the cinches for the second time explaining how horses will take a deep breath and hold it. This can leave the saddle loose and apt to fall off.

"Have either of you ridden before?" Bonz asked.

"I've never been on one." I said as I took a step back and pointed to Karen who had been given two years of riding lessons by her grandpa for a Christmas present when she was nine.

"It will give her self confidence." He had insisted when her parents disapproved. After months of discussion grandpa and Karen won out. Her fondest memory is of the first day when her grandpa lifted her up onto that magnificent animal the horse.

"Do you think you can get on or would you prefer to use our training aide?" Lean asked.

"I think I can manage," Karen said "but it's been so long I'm not sure I remember how to ride."

"Don't worry," Lean assured her as she held Apache in place "it's not quite like riding a bike but it will come back to you." In one cat like move Karen was in the saddle and Lean and Bonz quickly adjusted the stirrups to the proper length for Karen's long legs and then it was my turn.

I looked at how high the stirrup was and opted to use the training aide, which turned out to be a nearby rock. It was definitely not a smooth move that got me positioned in the saddle.

"Dreamer has been on a lot of these rides and will respond to the gentlest of commands." Bonz assured me as they tightened the stirrups to the proper length. "Pull gently on the reins, left one to go left and right one to go right. If you need to stop pull back gently on both. He should follow right along but a simple nudge with your foot will encourage him to keep up if he starts to lag behind." Bonz gave the instructions as if she had done it a million times.

"They have a natural pecking order." Lean explained as she and Bonz mounted their horses. "We find it easier to use it rather than trying to impose one of our own."

Dreamer was the easiest horse to maneuver but he was also last in line for the pecking order. I wasn't worried but hoped he would keep up without any nudging from me.

We headed through the trees along a narrow trail when we had a last minute addition to our group. Nez the young stallion had been left in the corral had jumped the fence and took his place as second in line. It would have taken a great deal of time to get him back into the corral so he was allowed to continue with us.

Dreamer swayed back and forth as he took slow steady steps. The horses stayed close together and seemed to be playing their own version of follow the leader, which included humoring the strangers who were along for the ride.

Suddenly the horses stopped and refused to go on for they had sensed a danger we could not see. We had a good laugh when we finally saw what had them worried. We were also more than happy to wait and keep our distance as a momma skunk and her two young ones hurried by.

Once we continued Lean and Bonz pointed out their favorite places on the ranch. "You can find a lot of fossils over there." Lean said pointing to an especially rocky area.

"I like this area here just because I think it looks neat." Bonz said to which I agreed.

We came to an open pasture where Nez really showed his stuff. Nostrils flaring and hair flowing he took off at a full gallop throwing his head from side to side. He seemed puzzled as to why his friends did not join him. Lean was quick to tell him, "You'll find out what it's all about soon enough Nez. It won't be long before we introduce you to the bit and a harness."

The others had gotten ahead of me when Dreamer must have decided it was time to head back to the corral. I tried to keep him from turning but nothing seemed to work. I pulled back on the reins to make him stop. This worked until he started walking backward which was more frightening than going forward had been. Karen hollered at me to ease up on the reins which had the desired effect, he once again stopped.

"Having trouble?" Karen laughed as she rode up next to me in full control of Apache.

"No matter what I did he kept turning." I explained.

Another lesson in left, right, stop, and we were on our way again being careful not to allow the gap to widen. Once I relaxed and was actually began enjoying myself we came to the end of the ride.

Lean and Bonz helped us dismount and then took the saddles off the relieved horse's backs. We didn't have to but enjoyed brushing the horses before they were released to roam freely on the ranch.

We then went to the cottage where we planned our itinerary for the day. Karen and I sat at the table while Lean made some fresh coffee and Bonz did a little tidying up.

"I think we should go fossil hunting first." I said rather insistent.

"I know," Karen said rolling her eyes. "You just can't wait to go play in the dirt and get in touch with mother earth."

"Exactly," I grinned from ear to ear at Karen, knowing she was looking forward to it as much as I.

"It's supposed to get really hot today," Bonz warned "so make sure you take plenty of water along."

"We didn't bring a canteen but if it's all right we can carry one of those gallon jugs." Karen replied.

"Of course, don't be surprised if Mariah follows along." Lean said smiling "She likes to make sure everyone gets back safely."

Bonz told us a shortcut to the area we had seen earlier and then she and Lean were off to do their daily chores.

We made our way through the bushes watching for snakes and any other dangers might be lurking nearby then spent the rest of the morning and part of the afternoon breaking rocks apart. We savored the fact that there were no visible signs of modern day man while Mariah watched over us as promised.

When we returned to the cottage we found other guests had arrived. A group of six sat around the fire pit. A member of their group eased the awkwardness of meeting strangers as she welcomed us back. "Bonz said you were out fossil hunting. Did you have any luck?"

"We found few muscles and plenty of shell fossils, however nothing to write the Smithsonian about." I smiled attempting humor to mask my own social inadequacies.

The one who had greeted us was heavy set with short brown hair, a warm smile, and welcoming eyes. She seemed to be the natural leader as she introduced the members of her group.

"I'm Iris and this is Rita my lover," she pointed to the slender woman next to her who seemed to be trying to hide behind her. "That's Helen in the Cowgirl hat and boots," at which everyone in the group giggled as if it were a private joke. She continued around the circle pointing toward each girl as she introduced her. "Lisa, Kathy, and Fran."

I followed her lead by only giving our first names as I introduced us. "Nice to meet you all, this is my lover Karen." at which I noticed Helen's smile fade as she kicked the dirt with her boot, "I'm Lynn and if you'll excuse us we need to freshen up before dinner."

"Of course," Iris agreed "We'll see you later."

As we neared the cottage we noticed there was another couple cuddling in the hammock oblivious to everything but each other. The slender redhead seemed to be about our age while the other had salt and pepper hair, which at least made her look a lot older. Not wanting to interrupt we walked by quickly and continued on to the cottage.

"I'm glad we got here yesterday." Karen smiled, "It was nice having the place to ourselves."

I smiled in agreement as I opened the cottage door. We showered and changed then joined the group back at the fire pit where wood had been stacked for the evening fire.

"How do you like the ranch so far?" Iris was again to first to greet us. It was easy to see why everyone here would be her friend and I suspect by the end of the weekend we would also consider her a friend.

Tonight's dinner would be Bar-B-Q Chicken, which would be cooked on the gas grill. The fire in the pit would be lit at dark and was more for atmosphere than out of any need for one.

After dinner the two who had been cuddling in the hammock excused themselves and headed for the cottage.

"Don't mind them," Irish said "their on their honeymoon."

"Honeymoon?" I questioned.

"They had a holy union this afternoon."

"A holy union, what's that?"

"A holy union is a religious ceremony performed by some churches. It's not legal but does give a sense of commitment to a relationship." Iris informed us.

"Interesting." I commented with my mind moving a mile a minute. I would have to find more on the subject later.

We sat around the fire telling stories about falling in love and relationships until the fire became nothing more than glowing embers. The others bid us good night then started heading for their cottages. I'd heard there were three but had no idea where the other two were. We headed for our cottage while Lean and Bonz made sure the fire was out before they could call it a night themselves.

As we entered the cottage we could hear the moans of passion coming from the other room. "Do you think they've been at it all this time?" Karen whispered.

"I guess anything's possible." knowing I could make love to Karen all night. "It might be a good time to do some star gazing." I said leading Karen back out the door.

"Let's try out the hammock." Karen suggested.

"Hmm good place to cuddle and do some stargazing from." I agreed putting my arms around Karen and pulling her close. A few kisses in the dark and we continued on to the hammock. I held the hammock steady while Karen lay down and once we were both on, it rocked from side to side until it slowed and stopped.

We closed the mosquito netting around us to keep the pesky things away then lay back as comfortably as we could. The sky was clear and it was easy to pick out the big and little dippers but both wished we knew more of the constellations.

We made a wish on a falling star then fell asleep in each other's arms. It was barely daylight when we woke to a hubbub of activity. Lean and Bonz were getting the horses ready for another ride while some of the women were anxiously waiting nearby.

"Well I see you two finally woke up." Irish greeted us in her usual cheery way as we laboriously got out of the hammock. "They've got room for one more on the ride if anyone wants to join in."

"We can go for a ride later." Karen said thoughtfully, "Until then we can find something we can both do."

"I'm stiff and sore in places I didn't know I could get stiff and sore." I said stretching slowly to emphasize my words. "I'm not going to be able to get on a horse today."

I could see Karen was looking forward to another ride and the thought of not going had chased the sparkle from her eyes. "Why don't you go without me?"

It didn't take her long to agree and we were soon at the corral where Rita, Fran and Helen in her cowgirl hat and boots were ready and waiting.

If I had known Helen was going on the ride I might not have been so insistent on Karen going without me. I had to mentally remind myself that I trusted Karen. After all what could possibly happen on a trail ride with so many others around? It was not easy to brush away the numerous possibilities that flashed through my mind as I tried to control the green-eyed monster stirring within.

I took a picture of Karen waving to me just before they disappeared into the trees and was ready for their return.

"They'll be back safe and sound soon enough." Iris said as if she sensed my concern. Little did she know it was not Karen's safety that had me worried? We walked back to the cottage and sat down near fire pit. From here we could see out over the ravines.

The moon still hung in the early morning sky but its glow paled as the sun continued to rise and take over. A hawk flew into the moon's path. This gave the illusion of his wings having a silvery accent before it suddenly dove earthward to some unseen target.

The air was cool and filled with the smell of honeysuckle, as the hummingbirds appeared to be rejoicing at the start of a new day. We sat in silence looking at the breathtaking view when Iris spoke. "It's so beautiful here. I wish I could visit more often."

I nodded in agreement. "Me too." After a few minutes I remembered that I wanted to ask her more about holy unions. I started uncertain of exactly what to ask. "You mentioned unions last night and I was wondering if you could give me a little more information?"

"What kind of information?" she asked.

"Well, this holy union thing," I thought for a moment then asked a barrage of questions all at once. "What are the requirements? What kind of ceremony is it? Who performs it? How do I get in touch with someone who will perform one?"

She laughed at all the questions then gave me what information she had "The answers to your questions will depend on which church you go to. Most of them want couples to have lived at least a year and insist on them going to some counseling sessions." She then asked, "You're pretty anxious about this. Does Karen feel the same?"

I answered as honestly as I could. "I asked her if she would marry me. I mean if we could. She never really answered the question but did say she wanted us to spend a lifetime together."

Wisdom showed in her eyes as she warned in a tone that seemed out of place for this normally cheery woman. "Sometimes you have to let it be enough. Don't push her to hard for one. I ruined a perfectly good relationship just last year by continually bringing up the subject of a holy union." She stared off at some unseen place that existed only in her heart then added, "She had a real phobia about making a long term commitment and eventually left me."

"I'm sorry if I brought up a painful memory." My heart went out to this big woman with an equally big heart as I felt her pain.

"It's good to remember the past. It keeps us from making the same mistake twice and might even help others if you know what I mean." she said seriously and I did understand what she meant. She wouldn't have shared this painful memory with me if she hadn't thought it might help.

We changed the subject and talked of less personal things such as work and school. She told me how she worked as an operator at a chemical plant near Houston and was excited when I told her I had an appointment for a job interview there next month. She was telling me whom to talk and to be sure to mention her name when the line of riders came by headed for the corral. We both followed them and I couldn't help notice how Helen who had been second in line when they left had moved into the position directly behind Karen.

By the time Iris and I arrived at the corral the riders had already dismounted and I noticed Helen whisper something to Karen as we approached. Karen smiled and nodded in agreement to whatever she had said. I tried to conceal my fears and greeted Karen warmly. When I was sure Helen was watching I gave Karen a big hug and a kiss that would make one think I hadn't seen her in weeks rather than mere hours. No one seemed more surprised by my actions than did Karen who looked at me as if I had gone off the deep end. I saw her questioning look and whispered, "I'll explain later."

When we went to our room to freshen up Karen immediately wanted to know, "So what was the big welcome back scene all about?"

"I just want to make sure Helen knows we are together and intent on staying that way."

"Why would you need to do that?" Karen asked as she sat on the edge of the bed.

"She's obviously very attracted to you." I pointed out.

"And what gives you that idea?" Karen laughed.

"Her look of disappointment was obvious when I introduced you as my lover. She watches every move you make when she can and she didn't waste any time making friends with you on the trail ride this morning and just what did she whisper to you just before I got there anyway?"

Karen didn't answer my question but insisted, "Your imagination is working overtime. She just wants to be friends."

"Maybe it is my imagination but I don't think so. She makes me nervous."

Karen got up and put her arms around my neck pulling me to her. Smiling she said "I think I like you a little nervous, now give me another one of those welcome back kisses."

I smiled back at her and was more than happy to fulfill her request. The heat of passion was building between us quickly cooled when a knock at the door was followed by the sound of Helen's voice. "Karen, when do you plan on leaving?"

I frowned at Karen's reply. "Will an hour from now be good for you?"

"I'll see you in an hour then." The sound of hopefulness in Helen's voice gave me an uneasy feeling again.

Jealousy was again trying to rear its ugly head as I asked, "You're not going without me?" It sounded more like an accusation than a question and when I didn't get an immediate response panic filled my voice, "Are you?"

"You sound like a child about to throw a tantrum." She accused.

"Do I have anything to throw a tantrum about?" I knew this line of questioning was insane but the words were out before I could stop them.

"This jealousy thing is beginning to get annoying. You know I wouldn't go without you. Now let's get ready and dress casual." She said having every right to be irritated with me. I couldn't help but feel there was something about this she wasn't telling me. We showered and changed in silence.

Helen was waiting for us and seemed to sense the tension in the air. Maybe it was the daggers in my eyes directed at her had caught her attention as she greeted us cautiously.

"Karen says you've wanted to go on a tour of the caverns. I couldn't talk anyone else into going and she said it would be all right for me to tag along but if it's not a good time I could stay here."

Hearing Helen confirm that my presence was always a part of the plan made me feel foolish. "You're more than welcome to join us." I assured her then turned sheepishly to Karen and whispered "Sorry."

Smiling as if she thought the whole thing was humorous, she took my hand in hers giving it a squeeze to let me know all would be forgiven.

The caverns were a couple of hours from the ranch. I was secretly happy that having the top down made it near impossible to have a conversation. It was cool inside the caverns, a natural phenomenon caused by the insulating effect of the earth. Helen shared my love of geology and we were soon discussing the mineral deposits and what might have caused the different formations to become what they are today. We both wondered what it would be like to find some undiscovered cave and be the first to explore it.

When the tour was complete Karen went off to browse the souvenir shop and while she was gone I took a closer look at our guest. It was no wonder I felt threatened by her. She wore a lavender shirt tucked neatly into a pair of tight fitting black jeans and a little wisp of blond hair hung from under her hat resting on the nape of her neck, all of which

I found quite appealing. I decided I had been foolish and took this time to apologize.

"I'm sorry I acted like such an idiot earlier. I thought you were attracted to Karen and I really let it get to me?"

"You weren't wrong." She said bluntly. "I am attracted to Karen but I would never do anything to break up a couple, happy or not." she was looking toward Karen who was turning the carousel searching for just the right post card.

"Did she say anything about being unhappy?" I asked.

"Quit" she scolded. "She seems very happy but be forewarned that if you ever break her heart I'll be more than happy to help her mend it." She winked.

Karen joined us with a very serious look on her face and an equally serious tone to her voice. "Is it my turn to be jealous?"

Panic filled me. Had she seen how I had been admiring Helen or could she somehow have sensed what had gone through my mind. Helen and I looked at each other dumbfounded as I answered defensively. "Of course not. You know better."

Karen still sounded quite angry. "I see, like the way you knew and trusted me." She smiled then winked at Helen.

I rolled my eyes and tried to laugh away the panic that filled me. "Yes I should have." I hung my head sheepishly. I wasn't going to be forgiven quite as easily as I thought.

"She got you with that one," Helen chuckled relieved to find it was just Karen's way of getting her point across "and you deserved it."

Pleased with herself Karen took us each by the arm and headed us toward the door. "You two have bored me long enough with all this talk about rocks."

"We weren't just talking about rocks." I defended.

"Say no more or I'll be getting jealous again." Karen teased but I couldn't help wonder if there might be a little truth to her words this time.

Our final evening at the ranch was spent telling ghost stories around the fire. Rita no longer hid behind Iris and joined in the fun by telling the old favorite one step, two step, three step I gotcha. I thought about retelling Paul's story of the marine then remembering my dream thought better of it.

The fire burned low and everyone seemed to be fighting sleep not wanting the night to end. I finally offered Karen a hand up and we gave everyone a hug good night, just in case we missed them in the morning. There was no sound coming from the honeymoon suite as we stumbled our way into the cottage. I think Karen was asleep before we got to the bed and I dozed off soon after.

When we woke in the morning the honeymooners had already left and others were getting ready to go. We packed our things and bid our new friends farewell. We vowed to keep in touch even though it was not very likely any of us would.

Even with all that had occurred it was hard to control my thoughts as Karen and Helen hugged goodbye.

CHAPTER 7

After our visit to the ranch, I was so intrigued by the thought of a Holy Union that I found myself thinking about it all the time. I knew we would have to wait until after graduation but wanted to start planning now.

Unsure of how she would react I decided to get as much information as I could before asking. A friend had told me of a church in the area that would perform the ceremony and I decided to start there.

Driving by on several occasions, I always found the church empty. It looked like any other church made of mortar and stone. In front a sign posted the hours of service along with the theme for next weeks sermon. "You are not alone." I would have to come back then to get the information.

When I returned people were milling about in their Sunday best. You would not be able to guess their lifestyle except for a few obvious couples and the rainbow sticker on many of the cars lining the nearby streets.

I had dressed to go in but for some reason could not and was about to pull away when I heard someone call my name. I looked around but did not see any familiar faces. When I heard my name again there was a woman waving in my direction. I could not tell who it was until she was standing next to the car.

"Hey Lynn," Kim called smiling as she neared the car. "Don't leave on my account." She hesitated then added "and don't look so surprised I told you I wasn't as rough around the edges as I look."

Kim, not looking the least bit rough around the edges had worn a pair of dress slacks and a delicate maroon shirt that added a warmth of color to her otherwise bland face. Of course the rough around the edges may have been the result of poor lighting and the smoke filled environment of the bar. Which, up till now had been the only place I'd seen Kim.

Still uncomfortable with the knowledge of her night of intimacy with Susan I could not find the right words. "I was just."

Unable to think of anything to say, Kim finished the sentence for me. A hint of sarcasm in her voice, "Driving by and saw all the queers standing around? Let me guess you were surprised to find out it wasn't a bar."

Her wit and obvious good humor eased the tension and I confessed, "Actually, I want to talk to one of the pastors about Holy Unions."

"You and Karen ready to make the big commitment?" she teased.

"I hope Karen will say yes." My uncertainty was obvious.

"You haven't discussed it with her yet?"

"Not really, I want to get all the information before I ask her."

"I'm sure she'll say yes." Kim smiled then asked uneasily, "How's Susan?"

"We haven't seen her much since the wedding but she seems to be adjusting to married life." I met her eyes and confessed. "She told me the truth about what happened between the two of you."

"She did, well good for her. I didn't think it was my place to tell you what really happened. You understand?"

"Yeah I did kind of put you on the spot and I probably would have done the same."

"I wish she'd have given us a chance." The pain behind Kim's words was deep.

"I think she wishes she could have too." I wasn't sure why I had said this for Susan had assured me that she married for love.

"I'm sure she might have given her marriage a second thought if it had been you," She said matter-of-factly her eyes locking onto mine, "but I was just a fling from the beginning." I began to feel uneasy once again when she offered. "Why don't you come in and I'll introduce you to the pastor after the service."

I felt as if destiny had intervened for why else would someone I hardly know show up just as I was about to pull away. Kim sat with me at the back of the chapel and after the service suggested we wait until the other churchgoers had filed by to thank the pastor.

I marveled at Kim who seemed so different as she introduced me. "Pastor Hudson, this is Lynn and she's interested in a Holy Union."

The pastor looked from Kim to me and then smiled at her.

"Not with me." She said wide eyed with terror and, her cheeks a delightful shade of red.

"Why is everybody always trying to pair me up? I like being single." She stepped past the pastor anxiously making her retreat.

"Thanks Kim." I called as she hurried away.

She merely waved without turning as she was going out the door.

"Kim is such a nice girl." The pastor commented after she had disappeared from sight.

I had misjudged Kim on our earlier encounters but could see now he was right. I smiled as I said, "Yes she is."

He led me to a small room barely big enough for the desk he sat behind. I sat on the other side expecting him to just give me all the information without any further hesitation.

He shuffled through a huge stack of papers on his desk and after what seemed like an eternity of silence spoke; "We prefer to have Holy Unions for members of our congregation." He said as he peered over his spectacles as if waiting for a reaction from me then continued as he handed me some documents "but it is not a requirement."

"We would like for you to attend at least one service and require a couple of visits with our counseling staff."

"Counseling staff?" I asked surprised.

"Nothing severe we just want to make sure you have been together at least a year and are both sincere about this commitment. They will want to meet with you together and separate. If we want the rest of the world to accept our Holy Unions we have to show it's more than just a piece of paper to those involved."

He watched as I looked over the papers he gave me and noted. "You seem very anxious about this."

"I can hardly wait to ask her." I said hopefully.

"I see. You haven't asked her yet?"

"No sir, I wanted to have all the information so I can answer any questions she might have."

"A wise plan and I hope all goes well for you both." He seemed anxious to be elsewhere.

"Thank you for your time Pastor Hudson and I hope to be in touch soon with some good news."

"We would like to see you both at service, anytime. Holy Union or not." He smiled.

I did not want to tell him how I had all but given up on churches. Not that I had given up on God but I do feel he has been evicted from many of today's churches. "We'll try" I said but was sure he could tell there was no conviction in my voice.

"God bless and keep you well." The pastor smiled warmly.

I smiled back. "Thank you pastor." Perhaps this church would be worth looking into for the pastor had sure made this sinner feel welcome.

I could hardly wait to face Karen with facts in hand when I asked her to marry me. We would have to wait until after graduation for the ceremony but I would ask her tonight.

Karen will be home any minute and everything must be perfect as I look around the room checking even the smallest detail. Ring box close to my heart, lights low with a candle waiting between two china plates and long stem crystal wine glasses all framed with real silverware. Some of Susan's wedding gifts I had borrowed for the night.

I meet Karen outside the door. "I have a surprise for you but I want you to shower and change before you see it."

"Mysterious." Karen smiled.

"Just close your eyes and I'll lead you to the bedroom."

"Oooh a surprise in the bedroom."

I laughed, "No now close your eyes and promise to keep them closed."

"OK I promise." Karen said with a mischievous grin.

I opened the door and led Karen as I watched closely to make sure she kept her eyes closed as promised through the living room and into the bedroom.

When I let her open them, she smiled and reached out to take me in her arms. "Your surprise smells delicious." She teased and pulled me closer.

"That's only part of it." I assured her. "Now get ready while I check on dinner and don't come out until I'm ready for you."

It wasn't long before Karen called out "What should I wear or are clothes optional."

Her teasing sent shivers through me. "Definitely casual but be forewarned that if you do come out in your birthday suit dinner will be ruined by the time you get a chance to eat it." The thought of Karen in her birthday suit set me on fire but I had planned this evening and could not let my desire for her take control, besides there will be plenty of time after I ask her.

"Are you ready yet?" Karen was getting anxious.

"Not quite." I replied as I lit the candle. I open the door for Karen who came in wearing jeans and a black sweater that fit like a glove. I hate when she wears this sweater in public but love seeing her in it and she knows it.

"That's almost as dangerous as your birthday suit." My voice was husky with want of her as I took her into my arms. The scent of her makes me weak.

We kiss tender at first then more demanding as our tongues intertwine, kindling the passion burning between us. My hands seem to have a mind of their own and start to roam when Karen pulls back a little.

"My surprise?" she asks looking out into the dark room with only the glow of candlelight to see by.

Karen walks past me. "Oh it's beautiful, just like a picture in a magazine."

Still drowning in a haze of desire I have to blink my eyes and clear my throat before I can move. I walk over to a chair and offer it to her. "Your seat my lady." The words roll off my tongue half in jest and half full of hope as she takes her seat.

I start a disk that I'd already loaded in the CD player. Classical guitar fills the room as a smile of approval comes from Karen. I serve dinner to my lady and myself along with a glass of wine, chilled of course.

Karen takes a taste of food then follows it with a sip of wine. "It's delicious but why so formal?"

"Special occasions deserve special attention."

"Is this a special occasion?" Karen leaned closer.

"I hope so." was my answer for I was not yet ready to divulge my secret.

"So mysterious, I'm intrigued." Karen sipped some more wine. "This is really exquisite wine."

"Only the best for my lady tonight." She looked puzzled at my choice of words but asked no questions.

After we finished our dinner we moved to the sofa where we enjoyed some more wine.

"All right," Karen insisted, "I've been patient long enough. What's this all about? What's the rest of my surprise?"

I take her hand in mine look into her eyes, and she laughs, "You look as if you're going to propose."

Doubt takes over as I look around the room quickly rethinking my plan. "I am. What I mean is I love you and want us . . ." In trying to catch up with my plan I attempt to pull the ring box from my pocket. I fumble sending the box flying across the room. I quickly retrieve it. The music stopped as I got to her side and I should have known then not to ask but I was a woman possessed sure everything would turn out all right once I said the words. "Karen will you marry me?" I opened the box and watched as the reflection of the small diamond glistened in her eyes.

The silence was merciless as my heart raced out of control. Karen had stopped laughing and appeared as though she were looking for a way to escape. Her expression was not the happy one I had expected.

I felt as if I were being ground into small pieces of dust as the realization of her coming answer hit me. "We can't marry its illegal, they won't let us." Karen's voice seemed panic stricken.

Still certain all would be well I tried to give her the information I had gathered. "I've checked it out and we can have a Holy Union at the HCC church."

"What is the point if it's not legal and what would the school say?" Karen sounded defensive and I wished I could start the evening over.

"We'll wait until after graduation." I said as my last glimmer of hope burned dim.

"I don't know I'll have to think about it for a while." She said staring blankly ahead.

My stomach felt as if a softball size rock were sitting in the middle of it as I searched for words to make everything OK. "It was a bad idea, forget it."

"I tried to understand what had happened as the night went on for what seemed like an eternity. We were suddenly strangers and feeling that it could get no worse I knelt beside her, took her hand in mine and asked, "What is the real reason?"

Karen turned away from me as she answered, "I don't know. Fear of commitment or something who knows?"

"Is that why you live with me, because you thought you'd never have to face commitment?" I asked as tears filled my eyes.

"It's not that I don't want to but there are so many problems . . . How would I tell my parents? Let's not talk about it anymore."

It was obvious that she was not going to discuss it more tonight. My heart sank knowing if we did not find a way to get past this our relationship was doomed. I held her close, "I still love you and we don't have to have a ceremony. I just thought you might like the idea."

We called it a night and went to bed. I knew it was even worse than it seemed when Karen turned her back to me without as much as a goodnight kiss.

I felt as if I were being drained of my very being leaving only an empty shell.

I leaned over and gave her a simple kiss on the cheek leaving her to her thoughts as I tried to sleep. I spent most of this night and many more wondering how to make things right as I watched her sleep.

$\mathcal{C}$HAPTER 8

Karen became distant and moody over the next few weeks. We would make love but it was quick almost dutiful then she would pull away and turn over. I missed drifting off to sleep and many times waking intertwined in each other's arms.

Every time I tried to bridge the gap Karen pulled further away and things only got worse. She was coming home later and finding excuses for not doing things together. I tried to forget it and convince myself it didn't matter as long as we were together. But Karen continued to change and it was soon obvious there was no going back.

As the holidays neared we had more and more disagreements and one day Karen announced that she was going to her parents for the holiday instead of making the trip we had planned together. I wanted to object afraid this time apart would put the final nail in the coffin of our relationship but with things the way they were it would have done more harm than good. I would have to believe in our love and give her the time she needed.

For the first time in my life I was dreading the coming of Christmas, although my mother was delighted to hear I would be spending this time with her.

I felt as if I had been handed a death sentence and each day only brought me closer. My heart was aching as I watched

Karen pack. She was taking almost everything that was hers, leaving only a few trinkets we had gathered together most of which I thought were more hers than ours.

When she had everything stacked by the door I could hold my tears no longer.

"You've packed everything! You're not coming back are you?"

She put her arms around me and I could see the love in her eyes but her words were not the ones I longed to hear, "I need some time apart to think"

"Think. I love you and I know you love me. What is there to think about?"

I searched her eyes for some sign of giving in but there was none. "I don't have to have a Holy Union. I just need you." I did not try to hold back the tears streaming from my face.

I thought she was going to say something when her arms slackened and dropped from around me. She turned and reached toward the door.

I could not let her leave without giving me some better reasons. As my hand touched her shoulder I was surprised to realize she was not reaching for the doorknob but instead for the lock which she clicked shut.

When she turned and put her arms around me again I practically knocked her over as I fell into them laughing and crying at the same time.

She started kissing me and we were soon devouring each other as we stumbled our way to the bedroom.

We made love like we had in the past. Slow passionate love for hours as we explored each other with a hunger that burns out of a true need for someone. I held Karen in my arms secure in the knowledge that she did love me as

I drifted into the deep sleep. Sleep had been avoiding me these past few weeks and I woke to the sound of a car door closing and the engine starting. When I realized Karen was not lying next to me, I jumped to my feet and raced to the window where I pulled the curtain back just in time to see Karen lift her head from the steering wheel and wipe a tear from her eye.

She must not have heard me calling for she pulled away without looking back. My hand was on the doorknob and the only thing that kept me from going after Karen was Susan's excited voice as she called my name.

"Lynn!!!!!!"

Still in a daze I turned toward her.

"What do you think you're doing?" she gasped.

"Going after Karen." I started to pull at the door.

"Well don't you think you should put some clothes on before you start running down the street?"

I think my whole body blushed when I realized all I was wearing were socks. "Damn." was all I could manage as I raced to the bedroom with Susan close behind.

I quickly slipped on a robe as Susan questioned me from the door. "What is going on? Why are you running out after Karen let alone naked?"

"Did she say anything to you before she left?"

"Just that she was going to her parents and you would be going to your mom's for the holiday."

"I don't think she's coming back."

"Of course she's coming back. Anyone who isn't blind can see how much she loves you."

"I don't think that's the issue. She has been upset ever since I asked her to have a Holy Union and our relationship has been going steadily downhill. Whatever the reason, she's gone and I'll probably never see her again."

"I was trying to get some answers from her last night when I thought she had changed her mind and was going to stay. I guess it was easier to make love then leave while I was sleeping then to leave me bawling at the door."

"You made love?"

"Yes sweet tender, and so full of passion. I felt so connected I never thought she would go, but she has."

"She'll be back as soon as she realizes what she's left behind."

"I hope so."

"She did say she would call you later."

I lowered my head and whispered, "Yeah" then we sat in silence for a while before I asked, "If you don't mind I would like to be alone?"

"I think I should stay."

"I am far from suicidal and I have to get ready to leave for mom's house anyway."

"All right but you have to promise to call me if you need anything, anything at all."

"And just where shall I call?"

Susan giggled "Oh we're going to his parents for Christmas. I'll call your mom's and give you the number later."

"O.K., I'll talk to you later then"

"You sure you don't want me to stay? You look terribly depressed."

"I'm sure." I said as I physically turned her toward the door and nudged her toward it. I longed to be alone.

"OK, OK I get the hint." She kissed me on the cheek a worried look on her face. "You take care"

"I will." I waved from the door a forced smile on my face as she drove away.

Once she had left I collapsed on the bed pulled Karen's pillow to me and cried till I could cry no more.

When I started packing I found a note . . .

Dearest Lynn:

> Please forgive me for leaving the way I did but I could not bear to see you cry. I need some time alone to think.
>
> I've been living in the here and now, not even considering what I might want for the future.
>
> Your request for a Holy Union has made me stop and think of lifetime plans. I know I love you deeply but I'm not sure I can give up entirely on the thought of a normal life with kids, dog and the old white picket fence. I must have time to think.
>
> Love Karen

So this had been the problem. Karen had been thinking of living the straight life. If it weren't so painful a thought I might have laughed, no wonder she couldn't tell me.

I could not picture it but knew many had forsaken their true feelings to live the fabled normal life. Whatever that is?

We would be spending this time apart because she could not bring herself to tell her parents. The outlook for our future was as the light of a candle flickering it's last in a gentle breeze.

I remember telling my mom who still insists it is just a phase then quickly changes the subject every time it comes up. She still pushes men my way in hopes I'll come to my senses.

Mom a small feisty woman not afraid to make her opinion known welcomed me with a big hug.

"Mom, you act as if you haven't seen me in years." I protest but hug her just as eagerly.

"It feels like it, anyway it's been a long time since you came for an extended visit."

"I know mom." Tears filled both our eyes as the hug ended.

"I've made up your old room." She headed me down the familiar hallway.

"Thanks mom." I went into the familiar room and put my bags near the bed. I noticed my mother frown and turn from the room as I reached in my bag, pulled out a picture of Karen and placed it next to the bed.

"I'll go fix dinner." She smiled weakly as she headed down the hall.

I hated being such a disappointment to her and understood what a powerful influence family acceptance could mean to a relationship. I was afraid Karen like Susan would not be able to tell her parents. That she would give in to their hopes and dreams for her. Hell what chance did I have when they were Karen's dreams too.

Karen had made it very clear I was not to call her and that she would call me as soon as she could. I missed her so much it was nearly unbearable waiting for her to call when she could talk freely. I found myself listening for the phone impatiently. Trying hard not to sound disappointed as familiar voices turned out to be relatives and not the one I longed to hear. When she did call she would suddenly hang up when someone came into the room on her end. No I love you, talk to you later, and not even a goodbye.

I missed her terribly and on Christmas Eve pleaded with her. "Let's go back early. New Years isn't really a family holiday. We should be together."

"I miss you to and I'll see if I can get away." She sounded uncertain.

I could feel the distance growing and knew I was powerless to stop it. I got angry. "I'm going back the day after Christmas. If you can make it I'll see you there. If not," My eyes stung with tears as I said words I did not mean. They burned in my throat, "don't bother coming back at all."

"I'll try." Came her muffled reply, which told me someone had come into the room on her end.

Tears streaming down my face I resisted the urge to slam the phone down only to have the line go dead as Karen hung up the other end. I was shaking as I put the phone back on its cradle.

My mother had entered the room and was quickly at my side. "There, there. You must love her very much?"" She said as she rocked me in her arms in an effort to comfort me.

"I do."

"I'll help you pack." She sounded determined.

I laughed through my tears. "But the family will be here tomorrow and I'm not going back until the day after tomorrow."

"You should go tonight. You should spend Christmas with the one you love."

My heart swelled at mom's sentiment "Thanks for the thought mom, but it's not that simple. Her parents don't know and Karen is afraid to tell them."

"Afraid of what? Afraid they will disown her or something?" she questioned.

"That is exactly what she is afraid of."

"You told me and I didn't disown you, now did I?"

"Almost and face it mom, you still hope I'll find some nice man and settle down."

"Well I'm an old woman and I look forward to having grand children."

"You have a dozen already." I laughed.

"Well with some things you can never have too many." She smiled.

"Let's see if you still feel the same tomorrow when they all visit at once." I teased as she left the room.

The next day was a hubbub of activity and Aunt Lynn as usual was surrounded by squealing toddlers being pulled this way then that. My sisters and the wives of my brothers had all gotten together and planned who would bring what so all my mother had to do was bake her wonderful pies. They also cleaned everything up before leaving with children in tow.

Once they were all gone I realized Karen had not called all day. I sat by the phone all night waiting for her to call.

Some time during the night mom had covered me with a blanket and I awoke to the sun shining through the curtains. Still the phone did not ring.

"Things will get better." Mom assured me as she said goodbye with another big hug.

"I hope so mom." I said still heartbroken that Karen had not called.

"If it doesn't work out I know a nice . . ." she started but stopped short when she saw the pained look on my face. "I hope it works out for you honey."

I knew what she really hoped but thanked her and promised to visit soon before leaving. "She can't help the way she feels any more than I can." I thought as I pulled away from the curb arm out the window waving.

CHAPTER 9

The apartment was cold and empty when I arrived. I don't know what had made me think Karen might be there but I had day dreamed of being greeted by her smiling face.

I turned up the heat and started unpacking when Susan called. "I thought you were spending the holidays with your mom."

"And I thought you were going to call." I said anxious to get off the phone still hoping Karen would call and say she was on her way.

"I did but you had already left." Susan tried to sound jovial but the worry was clear in her voice.

"I need to do some thinking of my own." I said flatly uncaring of a future without Karen.

"When your mother said you left early I was in hopes you and Karen had worked things out."

"Not really. I told her to make up her mind what she wanted and to be here by New Years or not bother showing up at all."

"You didn't."

"Yes I did and it is tearing me apart to think she might have believed I meant it. I can't go on like this, I'm falling apart but only Karen can make the final choice."

"If you want I can come back and keep you company."

"No, you bond with your in-laws and I'll be fine."

"I don't really fit in. All they seem concerned about is when are we going to have children as if that's all I'm good for."

"Yea good old normal married life just what you wanted." I had intended it to be humorous but there was a sharp edge to my tongue as I spoke the words.

"I'll let that pass because I know you're hurting but remember I am on your side."

"Sorry I didn't mean it the way it sounded. It will take time for them to get to know you and for you to know them. This isn't a good time maybe I should call you later."

She quickly gave me the number at her in-laws. "OK but I still don't think you should be there alone. Why don't you go out, meet some new people and forget about it for awhile."

Right I thought, it's such a trivial thing just forget about it. "I'll be just fine so stop worrying and I'll talk to you later." I hung up the phone before she got a chance to start again or before I lost control. Susan meant well but she couldn't really think going out to meet new people would help.

I was miserable the next week. Waiting by the phone not eating or sleeping except for passing out from time to time on the couch. The only calls were from Susan with a daily check up call.

After five days I could not even convince myself, as my voice crocked out the words. "I'm fine."

"That's it. I'm coming over." She commanded.

"No! OK so I'm not fine but I can take care of myself."

"Doesn't sound like it." She boomed.

"I'm just catching a cold. I'll be fine."

"I don't believe you."

"Susan you are over a thousand miles away. You can't just jump in your car and come check on me. I'll be fine, really."

"If you don't sound better tomorrow I'm coming home."

"You are worse than my mother."

"If you don't take care of yourself your mother and I will both be there and if I had Karen's number I'd call her too. She should know what is happening to you."

"You wouldn't"

"Yes I would."

"Oh all right already. I promise to take care of myself."

"It's New Years Eve and I want you to go out and have a good time."

"Today is New . . . already?"

"Yes and don't you dare stay home alone."

"I might as well go out I guess." There was no conviction in my voice. "There's no reason to sit here waiting. She hasn't called all week. There's no reason to think she will show tonight."

This seemed to satisfy Susan who wished me a happy new year before hanging up. Dizzily I pulled myself off the couch and headed for the kitchen. There was nothing here to eat and I would have to take a shower before going out.

I blinked at the reflection staring back at me from the mirror. I looked awful. My eyes were sunken, while my hair dirty and unkempt framed my pale tear stained face. To bad it's not Halloween I could go as I am I mused to myself. Susan was right I couldn't continue this way.

I got myself cleaned up and noted the vast improvement over just a few moments ago. It was 8:30 by the time I headed out to the bar.

I stopped at a drive through for a quick bite knowing that if I waited to long the bar would be standing room only. My eyes filled with tears as I thought of how Karen and I had made reservations back in October so sure we would be spending this night together.

I pulled into the parking lot where it was filling up quickly. I sat in my car as I tried to finish the burger and fries I had just bought. For what seemed like an eternity I watched happy couples flood the bar to over flowing.

I couldn't do it. I could not bear the thought of spending tonight of all nights at the bar without Karen. My mind raced with wild thoughts what if she went to the apartment and I was not there? What if she is at the apartment waiting for me now?"

I started the car and raced back to the apartment, my heart and mind once again full of hope, only to find it dark and empty. The only light was the one blinking like crazy on the phone machine. I locked the door behind me, flipped on a nearby light and eagerly pushed the play button only to hear the voices of friends and family as they got an early start wishing all a Happy New Year. I could hear party noises in the background of most of the calls. The happy sounds made me feel empty and alone. I would have fallen apart in public so it was good I had come back to the apartment.

After the last message had finished and none of them from Karen, I asked out loud to no one yet everyone. "What is so damn happy about it any way?"

Holding back tears I fixed myself a good stiff bourbon and coke, not my usual drink but it would do for tonight. The drink was so strong I nearly choked on the first sip. I weakened it just a bit then turned on the TV to watch the festivities being broadcast from the downtown Hyatt where all the big wigs in their formal attire had gathered together to welcome the New Year.

With the phone by my side and plenty of bourbon and coke I watched agonizingly as they counted down the hours, only three more and still no word from Karen. I fixed my fourth drink and realized I was already having trouble negotiating my way back to the sofa.

No problem, I'll just put some ice in the igloo and bring the drinks closer. I smiled at my own genius, a sure sign I was well on my way to being totally bombed. Perfect by midnight I wanted to feel nothing, absolutely nothing.

Several drinks later I watched blurry eyed as they did the final countdown.

10 more seconds and my life would be over
9   I sit with my hand on the phone
8   I will call her and wish her well
7   I can't give in
6   Please ring
5   I gulp down the last of my 8th no 10th drink.
4   "Oh fuck who gives a shit anyway?"
3   Damn it ring!
2   "Karen how can you do this to me?"
1   "I love you so much"

HAPPY NEW YEAR

Noisemakers and fireworks went off everywhere but I did not hear them. The alcohol had done its job, dulling my senses to the point of passing out. My head was so heavy I could not lift it. "Was that the phone?" In reaching for it I missed completely and ended up laying half on and off the sofa.

My head was spinning so much I had no control over any part of me. I closed my eyes and everything went black.

My head was pounding when the phone rang again bringing me back to a semi conscious state. I brought the receiver to my ear and barely managed, "Hello" as my tongue was so dry it stuck to the roof of my mouth.

Susan's voice boomed bright and cheerful, "HAPPY NEW YEAR", which almost caused me to drop the phone. After no response from me she asked. "Did you have a good time last night?"

I could not answer. Water, I needed water. With the phone still to my ear I stood to go to the kitchen. The sudden dizziness was too much for me, my knees buckled and luckily I landed back on the sofa.

"Lynn, are you all right?" Susan sounded frantic.

"OK, caaaan't talllk rigght now. Calll you lattter." The words stuck in my dry mouth.

"I see. Someone had too much to drink last night. Say no more I'll check on you later, take care."

All I could manage was a grunt then hung the phone gently back on the cradle. No noise, please no noise but even thought caused an unbearable pounding in my head which I let sink back onto the sofa wanting only to pass out again.

My eyes suddenly opened no longer concerned with the severe pain that the light was causing them. Where had this pillow come from? It was not here last night, or was it.

Last night, let's see, lots of drinks, with many trips to the bathroom but definitely no pillow. Then again, there is so much about last night I don't remember. I attempted to get up but my legs went wobbly, until now I thought falling down drunk was just a phrase.

I steadied myself, took two steps. The room spun, I closed my eyes, which only made it worse. My knees once again gave way and I was soon on the floor. I had to get to the kitchen and unable to stand I started crawling.

Suddenly I felt the whole room spinning I reached out and found exactly what I needed. I pulled a small trashcan to me just in time to heave a great deal of liquid into it, oh how it burned my throat. What ever made me think that drinking so much alcohol could ever make me feel better?

My head steadied a little but I did not try to stand. I opted to continue crawling my way to the kitchen. It felt as if I had crawled across the entire Mohave Desert rather than just a few feet across the living room to the kitchen. I was grateful for the coolness of the tile and lay there for a few moments before trying to stand.

Although my body was shaking I managed to pull myself up to the sink. I turned on the cold-water. I cupped my hand under the wonderful flowing liquid and splashed some on my face. My mouth ached for relief but I knew better than to drink to fast. I cupped my hand under the faucet and drank. I drank from my hand as if at desert oasis with no other container available.

I was feeling better and reached for a glass. I knocked one to the floor where it shattered with an unforgiving sound that rocked my aching head. I would have to clean it up later but right now I had to have more water. I clutched another glass into my shaking hand and filled it to the brim.

I brought it to my parched lips and sipped slowly. The water filled my mouth and trickled down my throat inside and out. I had never known that mere water could bring such relief or pleasure.

I splashed more water on my face, closed my eyes and was taking another sip when I started shaking so violently

I spilled water all over myself. I felt the room spinning and knew I was about to fall again.

I felt an arm go round my waist and as much as I wanted to I could not open my eyes to the spinning room. Somehow I knew it was, "Karen" I sighed with relief.

"Yes Lynn" Her voice was so sweet to my ear.

I smiled then grabbed the sink and again hurled some noxious liquid from my now aching stomach. I felt a cool rag on my forehead as Karen held me up.

"Karen, is it really you?" I managed before heaving again. Dry heaves this time, which made my stomach, feel as if it would be forced from my body.

"Stop trying to talk. We can do that when you feel better."

Once I felt a little steadier she helped me to the sofa and lowered me gently. "Lynn, how much did you drink last night?"

"Why didn't you come home last night?"

"Never mind that now, just rest." Karen nursed me for several hours and I held on tight now afraid she was a hallucination that would somehow disappear if I let go.

Finally Karen spoke, "I'm sorry Lynn I should have been here last night. I was on my way out the door when mom stopped me."

"Is that why you didn't come home? You know I didn't mean it. You're here now, to stay?" I asked almost pleading.

"Yes" No maybe, no excuses, no it can't be, just a plain and simple yes. I was so happy I wanted to dance but my spinning head would never allow such an activity so I pulled her to me and held her close instead.

"I told my mother." Karen stated as if that explained all.

"Really?"

Karen smiled, and brushed my hair from my face. "Really, she wanted to know why I was leaving early and

I was so tired of lying that I simply told her the truth." I listened intently as she continued. "Once I started I said it quickly so I could not change my mind before telling her all."

"What was her reaction?" I said overcoming my spinning head as I sat up to listen.

"She looked at me with that knowing look all mothers seem to have and said,

We wondered when you would get around to telling us.'" She looked relieved as she continued. "They don't hate me or want to disown me. I am their daughter and they love me. Nothing can change that."

I smile at her, for she has been delivered from the darkness that had threatened our love.

"All the agony I put myself through when they knew all along. I never dreamed they had already figured it out. They were trying to make it easy on me by waiting for me to tell them."

"I've missed you Karen." I smiled.

"I've missed you too." Karen leaned forward and kissed my forehead.

Damn what a time to suffer from alcohol poisoning. "Lynn," she looked into my eyes.

"Yes?"

Her next words made my heart soar. "Do you still want to marry me?"

"Of course I still want to," I pulled her closer. "I want nothing else."

My heart and mind wanted to make love but all I could do was curse my spinning head and aching stomach for being able to do no more than hold her close.

CHAPTER 10

Holy Union:

Karen's parents insisted on paying for the entire ceremony. Her mom had been planning Karen's wedding since before she could walk and was delighted to find out we wanted as close to a traditional ceremony as possible.

Every detail had been planned for months. Still when the day finally arrived I was in a panic, sure some important detail had been forgotten.

I was wearing a white tux when my mother picked me up and drove us to the church. Karen was in the church getting ready and people had already begun entering the chapel.

We sat in the car for a few moments then mom put her hands on mine in an attempt to steady them. "Relax dear." She smiled.

"I can't mom, I'm a wreck. I just know I'm going to blow the whole thing." My voice was almost as shaky as my hands.

"You'll do fine. Just remember you love her and you know that she loves you, the rest of us you don't need to worry about."

"I'll try mom." My voice still trembled.

Since Karen's parents paid for the wedding, my mom insisted on giving us a surprise honeymoon. She was very secretive only saying, "Pack casual with maybe one nice outfit. Trust me you'll love it."

Before we went into the church she handed me an envelope. "Things will be hectic later so I'll give these to you now."

I opened the envelope and glanced at a brochure for a seven-day five-night Caribbean cruise. I always heard about cruises being a great place to meet men. Just what we need an entire week on a ship full of Don Juan want to bes.

I tried to hide my disappointment as I put it back inside the envelope, "A cruise, how wonderful. Karen will love it." I tried to sound convincing as I leaned forward to kiss my mom on the cheek.

She knew me to well and put her hand up to stop me. "Don't be in such a hurry to assume the worst. Look at the brochure a little closer."

I pulled it from the envelope, turned it over then opened it. A smile spread across my face as I looked into my mother's eyes, which were beaming with pride. "That's right, it's a special all lesbian cruise. You'll be able to walk about the boat arm in arm. That is if you leave the cabin." She smiled.

"Oh mom!" I gave her a big hug and the well deserved kiss on the cheek.

"We'd better get going. We don't want to keep Karen waiting." She insisted as she pulled from my grasp and climbed from the car.

We went in and were greeted by friends and family. They where wishing me well and telling me how lucky I am as I made my way to the front of the room. I took my place next to Carl who had agreed to be my best man so to speak. I was going to ask Susan to stand with me but she was so eager to be a bridesmaid I asked Carl.

His voice seemed to be mocking when he commented. "And they said we would never do it."

"Do what?" I had no idea what he was talking about.

"You and I in front of a priest, they said it could never happen." He laughed and I laughed with him.

Five minutes seemed like an eternity as we stood there waiting for the pastor to arrive.

"Sorry another ceremony took longer than expected." He explained.

"No problem." I smiled nervously back at him.

The music started and I turned to watch Karen walk down the aisle. When she came into view it took my breath away. She was so beautiful in her old fashioned wedding gown with the long train. Her cousin Geri as maid of honor followed close behind, then Susan and three other bridesmaids in pale blue dresses.

With each and every step my heart beat faster. Once she was beside me I took her hand in mine and we turn to face the pastor.

He started in the loud clear voice of someone who had done this many times before. "Dearly beloved we are gathered here today to witness the pledge of love between Lynn and Karen. Their decision to commit to a shared lifetime of troubles and joys was not take lightly and should be looked on with a great deal of respect."

"They have written their own vows and will exchange rings as a token of their undying love. Lynn if you would please begin."

My heart immediately jumped to my throat and I was sure no sound would come forth when I attempted to speak. I turned and gazed at Karen's face, her veil was short and I could see her eyes clearly. It was there that I found the strength to speak the words I had been practicing all week.

My voice trembled as the words found their way from my heart and tumbled from my lips. "I Lynn, who loves you more than life itself promise you a lifetime of love and I want you to know I will do everything in my power to help you make all your dreams come true." I smiled knowing half of what I wanted to say was still bouncing around inside my throbbing head. I tried to say more as my mouth moved but no sound emerged. I signaled that I was finished by clumsily slipping the ring on her finger.

"And Karen" the pastor prompted.

Her hands trembled as she slid the ring on my finger. Her voice was shaky,

"I Karen pledge my undying love to Lynn and am so glad she did not give up on me when I made life so hard on her. When I think of how I almost threw our love away because of the way things are supposed to be."

Pain filled my heart when I saw the tears in her eyes. "I'm here." I whispered, "We're here" I said squeezing her hand in mine. "We have our whole lives ahead of us." That was just a small part of what I had forgotten to say.

"I love you so much," She bubbled nearly crying, "and I'll never let you go again."

I was about to take Karen into my arms when I heard the pastor say, "You may now kiss your life partner."

We had promised each other a short peck to make it easier on any of our guests who may not fully understand our relationship. However as I took her in my arms I knew that would not do and I kissed her long and hard as she responded with the same.

"Save some for later." I heard someone call out.

Our lips parted slowly and our eyes locked. As I released her we turned to face the crowd. We were both smiling outrageously as the pastor presented us to the world. "I present to you Life Partners Lynn and Karen. May their love continue to grow."

I was so relieved when it was over I nearly collapsed as we took our first step. Good thing Karen was there to keep me from falling over. Nothing had really changed we were the same people we were fifteen minutes ago. Only the piece of paper acknowledging our commitment was new. A small piece of paper that was only legal in our hearts and yet inside I felt a lot different. I felt a joy I had never thought possible and was sure that now we could face anything life had to throw at us.

The reception was pure chaos. So many people there to wish us well. We did the whole nine yards. They even had two brides on the cake. I wonder where they found one in a tux.

I tenderly offered Karen the first bite of wedding cake and in return I got a face full of cake and icing. When it came time to exchange sips of champagne I was wary but not a drop was spilt.

I knelt down and took the garter from Karen's leg and tossed it toward a group of waiting young men and women. A lanky young man I did not know claimed the prize and stuffed it in his pocket.

Karen threw the bouquet to a throng of giggling young ladies. It bounced up a couple of times, broke into four pieces, and a different girl claimed each piece. The whole room filled with laughter and it was time for us to go.

I had one last surprise for Karen, two huge heart shaped balloons filled with helium. One had Karen's name on it and the other of course had mine. I released them, "I set these balloons free to intertwine as they face whatever the world can throw at them."

"Just like us." Karen smiled as they sailed away.

"Yes" I gently kissed her and then we watched as the balloons sailed higher and then finally out of sight.

Rice in our hair and alone at last we drove to the airport. We drew a lot of double takes as people realized there were two women in the car marked, Just Married. We smiled and waved at the drivers who honked to wish us well.

The cruise was wonderful and we even managed to come out of our room a couple of times. One was at night to do some stargazing. There were no lights for hundreds of miles and the stars shown like thousands of tiny suns, filling the sky.

Just before the moonrise they turned off all but the running lights on the ship so all on deck could experience the full effect. It only took a few minutes but I was awestruck from the moment it first started to come into view. It seemed so close that I actually reached out and tried to touch it.

CHAPTER 11

Five years have passed and we are still living happily ever after. We finished dinner and just said goodbye to Carl and Frank who are still together and have become part of our family.

Karen was literally glowing as she watched Mary 3, named partly after me, and Jr. 2, as they play happily on the floor. It would not be long before Susan and Roger would be by to pick them up.

We had started baby sitting Mary when she was just 2 weeks old and have become known as Aunt Karen and Aunt Lynn. The nights of babysitting had started out great, changing, feeding, rocking them to sleep, and then sending them home with mom and dad.

A little over a year ago they began sending Karen into a deep depression that would last for days. Her depression had gotten so bad that I had to insist Susan find a new baby sitter. However now thanks to modern medicine and a small donation from Carl, we are now expecting our own child.

Carl had been unsure at first; even though we assured him we would take full responsibility. We would not expect any more from him than the necessary sperm.

Two weeks had passed when he came to us ready to accept our proposal on one condition. He wanted to be a part of the child's life, even if it was only as Uncle Carl.

"We intend to be as honest as possible with the child but we don't want you to be known as Uncle Carl." I insisted.

A dark look came across his face as he stood to go. "I can't do it then."

He was at the door so quickly I thought he would be gone before I could stop him. "Wait," I called as Carl was reaching for the door. He stopped and turned to face us.

"I will not change my mind." He said forcefully.

I could hardly keep from laughing as I clarified our position. "We would prefer to have the child call you daddy, that is," I hesitated, "if you don't mind."

A smile came across his face unlike any I had ever seen before. The sparkle in his eyes seemed double what it had been. "I'd love to be daddy but I thought you wouldn't want me involved at all. You know, anti men and all."

"We've never been anti men." I defended. "How could we have remained friends all these years if we had been anti men? Are you and Frank anti women?"

Laughingly Carl answered "No, well at least when it comes to you and Karen anyway."

It had taken three months of trying for the artificial insemination to be successful and now we only had two months to go before the big event.

Frank had been against the whole thing at first. "It's not right" was his unending plea to Carl. Once the baby was conceived he saw how happy we all were, and it was contagious. Frank an avid shopper had soon supplied us with everything we would need and then some for the baby.

My mother had passed away but I know she would have been pleased to have one more grandchild. Karen's parents who had resigned themselves to the fact, they would have no grandchildren where thrilled with the news.

Carl and I both went to Lamaze with Karen. "It will be good to have a back up." He had insisted.

We decided it would be best for Karen to give up teaching for now and become a full time mother.

I had taken a job at a chemical plant just outside of Houston and was out of the office when Karen called. I had taken the little pink message slip from my mailbox upon returning and was trying to make out the secretaries handwriting. She came around the corner smiling.

"You'd better get going." She beamed.

"Going?"

She pointed to the message slip. "It's from Karen. She's on her way to the hospital."

"Oh shit!" I said as I ran for the door. My co-workers were well aware of my relationship with Karen. It was one of the main reasons I had come to work for this company when so many others had made better offers. It was owned and operated by two men who just happened to be life partners.

An added bonus was that Karen and the baby would be covered by my insurance. This made it possible for her to become a full time mother like she wanted.

I was hurrying to the hospital running all red lights until a close call caused me to slow down. Better to get there late than not at all.

I slipped on the mask and gown before entering the room. Karen was in full labor and would deliver any minute now. Carl looked peeked and seemed very relieved when I arrived. Karen screamed out when another contraction caused her great pain. She squeezed my hand with such a vice like grip that I was afraid it might break a few bones.

This was more than Carl could stand and he went to the waiting room.

Before I could coach Karen on her breathing I heard the doctor say, "I can see the head. It won't be long now." My heart was beating so fast I was sure I would faint.

With the next contraction Amanda Lynn came into this world. Covered in goo, the umbilical still attached she let out a scream to let us know that she was not as happy about this event as we were.

Everyone in the room let out a short laugh, the kind that comes at the end of a tense moment. I kissed Karen on the forehead as the doctor announced, "Congratulations it's a girl." I got to cut the cord then she was taken over by a nurse. Karen and I held each other as we watched the nurse clear Amanda's nose and mouth. She put drops in her eyes, washed her and placed her in a warm blanket, which seemed to calm her.

Karen didn't even seem to notice as the doctor finished up, removing the afterbirth. She was allowed to hold the baby a little, before being wheeled back to her room for rest.

I know it was probably caused by gas or something but I'll always remember the way she smiled at me when I first took her in my arms. I marveled at the ten tiny fingers and the ten little toes as I gave thanks for the miracle I held in my arms.

Amanda went to the nursery, Karen to her room where I would join her after checking on Carl. He was in the waiting room, handing out cigars to everyone like any proud papa would.

The next few years were full of firsts with a closet full of photos to document each of them.

First day home, exciting.

First all night of sleep, heavenly.

First crawl, into everything.

First tooth, agony for us all.

First birthday, enough toys from friends and family to supply a day care.

First steps, and we thought it was hard to keep up with her before.

First word, we had coached her on mama for months. Wouldn't you know it one day Carl showed up and was greeted with dada?

First day of school, though Amanda loved it, Karen was apprehensive.

First works of art are some of my most treasured possessions.

First time the question we had been expecting to come up was asked from Amanda's special point of view. It was not why mommy and daddy don't live together but rather, ""Why doesn't everyone have two mommies and daddies?" As if she wouldn't have it any other way.

We had rehearsed it so many times and yet were taken by surprise. Oh how to explain to a six year old. "You were what children were meant to be, the essence of our love. Not only mine and your mothers, but also of your daddy's and Frank's."

It was clear she did not understand what her mother was trying to explain and this more detailed explanation would have to wait a few years. "Because you my dear are special and have enough love for four." Karen smiled. As she placed a finger on the tip of Amanda's nose.

She hugged us both and kissed our cheeks before running off to play with Susan's kids who had become like siblings to Amanda.

First boyfriend, we met at parent's night third grade.

Finally and most dreaded of all, First trip to the emergency room.

All Karen could manage was "get to the hospital now." I had called Carl before leaving work and though he had twenty more miles to drive we arrived at the same time. We were greatly relieved to find nothing was broken, only a sprain to be kept in a sling for a few weeks.

Years later we explained how she was the essence of our love. How many children were the unplanned result of some fling and sometimes unwanted. How she had been planned and was truly the result of our love. It is a part of who you are and you have four people who love you more than life itself.

CHAPTER 12

Time went by as quickly as grade school turned to middle then high school. It was hard to believe Amanda would soon be graduating from high school with honors. We were preparing to celebrate her eighteenth birthday when I received a hysterical phone call from Frank.

His words came in spurts "Carl's . . . in . . . in . . . the . . . hospital." he sobbed uncontrollably.

"Which one?" I tried to ask calmly but knew my voice was clearly giving way to panic.

Between sobs he managed to get out the name of the hospital.

"Frank, what happened? Is he going to be all right?" I asked but it was obvious that he had held up as long as he could for all he did now was sob into the phone."

"We're on our way." I assured him before hanging up. Amanda and Karen had overheard and were already headed for the car.

We drove to the hospital in silence not wanting to contemplate the possibilities that flashed through our minds as if saying them might make them true. No amount of speculation could have prepared us for the truth. Carl had been the victim of a hate crime. He had been beaten and shot. He was not expected to live.

We sat in a small private room as we waited for news. I kept my thoughts to myself for I had waited in a private room like this when my father died and knew it must be serious.

When the doctor came in, his expression was grave. I wanted to be able to shield Amanda from what I was sure he would say. I knew I could not, any more than my mother could shield me when my father had died of a cerebral hemorrhage.

I took her hand in mine expecting the worst. I was so overpowered by relief, when the doctor said, "He's alive." I almost missed the rest of what he had to say.

"He has sustained sever internal damage. They obviously hit and kicked him repeatedly, then shot and left him for dead. Ironically the gunshot wound only caused minor damage."

My relief turned to anger as the thought of Carl being kicked, beaten, shot and left to die in the filth of a gutter by a group of boys filled my head. Boys trying to prove what great men they will be and still we are the ones that society fears.

I turned my attention back to what the doctor was saying, "If Frank hadn't been there to call for help he would have died right were they had left him. As it is he still only has a 50-50 chance. He's in a coma and is on life support for now. He may not come out of it and had left instructions in his living will that he does not wish to be kept alive with machines."

All we could do was look unbelievingly at the doctor who continued, "However he does not stipulate how long to wait so that will be left up to you. In any case he will be given time to show improvement."

After a moment of silence he asked, "Do you have any questions?"

"Would a transplant of some kind help?" I asked hopefully.

"I don't think that will be possible in his present condition." He looked around the room at the solemn faces then politely excused himself and left.

Once the doctor was gone Frank began to sob. I took him in my arms to comfort him but he pushed me away. "It's my fault."

"No Frank it was not your fault." I tried to assure him.

"Yes it is." He paced in quick jerky movements.

"Can you tell us more about what happened, Frank?"

His eyes glazed over as he started "Carl did not want to go out but I persuaded him to come." he paused so long I didn't think he was going to say anymore.

"That does not make you responsible for what those punks did Frank."

He shook his head no, gritted his teeth and continued, "There's more to it. We had left the bar and were heading for the car when they came out of the alley. They surrounded us. Momma's boy they kept calling as they walked in a circle around us. Occasionally they would take a swing at us without making contact, taunting us. One of them pulled out a gun."

He took a deep breath and wiped away the tears before continuing, "Carl pushed me through the group of boys yelling for me to run. I did heaven help me I ran but . . . I . . . I thought he was right behind me." Tears streamed down his face now as his words became almost inaudible. "I'm the momma's boy it should have been me. It should have been me." He collapsed against the wall and sank to the floor.

There is no way to help someone face a pain that cut so deep and all I could do was once again put an arm around Frank for comfort as he told the end. "I had run nearly three blocks before I looked around and saw Carl was not there. By the time I got back to him they were gone. They left him so bloody that if I had not been there when it started I would not have known it was Carl. I ran to the bar and called for help."

"There's no way you could have known Frank it's not your fault."

He said no more only wept as I held him.

Frank was at the hospital every moment they allowed and the only way we could get him to eat was to convince him he had to keep up his strength for when Carl awoke.

We visited Carl's bedside daily. After the initial shock of seeing his swollen face, we watched for any sign of improvement.

A week had passed when I received a call from the hospital saying Carl was awake and wanted to see us. I picked up Karen and Amanda on the way and we happily raced to the hospital.

We were attempting to get past a nurse who was insisting only one at a time could visit when the doctor arrived and shooed her away. Without a word he opened the door and held it for us to enter.

I was surprised to see all the tubes still attached as we crowded into the small cubical. The still beeping monitors made it hard to get close to Carl but with Karen and Amanda on one side and Frank and I on the other we managed to get close enough.

Carl's eyes were weak but determined as he looked at each one of us, smiling at his beloved Amanda. When he first spoke it was to her. "I want you to know how very much I love you."

Tears filled her eyes and she would have hugged him if it had been possible. I could tell he wanted to hold her as well. His eyes watered and tears rolled down his swollen cheek when she replied. "I love you too daddy."

He looked to us as he spoke again so weak we could barely hear him. "Promise to take care of our girl." But before we could answer his eyes closed and the monitors started buzzing loudly. We backed away from the bed to make room for the doctor who had raced into the room.

The doctor checked Carl, turned off the buzzing machines then turned to us and grimly said. "I'm sorry he's gone."

"What do you mean he's gone?" I questioned. "He had come to we thought it meant he was getting better."

"I'm sorry if I said anything to mislead you when I called. His internal injuries where just too severe and he took a turn for the worse last night. I didn't think he would make it till morning and suggested you be called."

I looked to Frank who was already crying as he explained. "I'm sorry I know I should have called but I felt it would be giving up and I didn't want to admit he was . . . dying." He said the word then fled the room.

The doctor spoke again, "I was truly amazed when he woke up this morning. He must have had something very important to tell you."

I looked toward Amanda who was crying as Karen held her close. Knowing how much we had lost, my words hung in my throat. "It was" I hesitated, "the most important thing anyone can ever say." I walked over to Karen and Amanda and wrapped my arms around them both. We held each other tight as we cried.

It was no surprise Carl had prearranged everything years ago. It was a surprise to find out he had planned so far ahead that he had purchased a double deep plot for him and Frank, a double deep plot for Karen and I, with a plot in the middle for Amanda in case anything happened to her before she could make plans of her own.

He even bought a headstone to cover all three. It had an angel in the center with wings that spread out to each side. I was touched he wanted us with him through all eternity. After some minor discussion decided we all liked his plan to keep our family together.

The funeral was solemn as friends and family paid their last respects. The room was filled with flowers and the mixed aromas stung my senses making me nauseous. To honor his wishes we had a closed casket with a picture of his smiling face set before it.

Carl having lost many friends to aides recently did not like funerals. He hated it when others would say how good the person looked. "He doesn't look good he looks dead." He would say tearfully the pain clear in his eyes.

Amanda spent most of her time with Carl's parents hoping to ease their suffering. Seeing so much of him in her must have helped ease their pain. Before heading to the graveside service Carl's mother hugged Amanda possessively. She stated, "I'm so glad we have Amanda." I felt a chill as the hairs on the back of my neck stood up. I felt like a mother bear suddenly needing to protect a cub. It was all I could do to keep from pulling Amanda from her grasp.

I'd read about the grandmother in Virginia who had gained custody of a grandchild because the mother lived with another woman. It must have been an ugly custody battle. Thank God, Amanda is eighteen.

I had never thought to ask Carl what his parents' thought of our arrangement and now I would have to ask Frank.

"Frank," I whispered, "did Carl ever tell you how his parents felt about our decision to have Amanda?"

Frank glassy eyed shook his head clear of some faraway thought then answered, "They were like me. At first they disapproved but couldn't help love her from the moment they laid eyes on her."

"What did they have to say about me and Karen raising her?" I asked.

"She gave Carl a hard time saying that allowing their grandchild to be raised by a couple of lesbians was unacceptable. She wanted him to let her sue for custody and raise Amanda herself."

"Why didn't he ever tell us?"

"He didn't want to worry you needlessly."

"Needlessly," my voice raised an octave or two and people looked our way.

"Don't get so excited it's all in the past Carl knew how to control his mother. He was the only one who ever could." Frank sighed then continued, "Carl put an end to it by letting her know he and Karen would get married if that is what it took to stop her and then she would never see any of them ever again."

"I can't believe he never told us of this possible threat."

"Why are you so worried about it now anyway?"

"I'm sorry Frank, but even though it is not a threat now it scared the hell out of me to think of what could've happened."

"As long as we are talking about Amanda I need to know something."

"Sure." I looked at him questioningly.

He almost whispered his question. "Will it still be O.K. for me to come over and visit?"

Without hesitation and quite surprised he had felt the need to even ask, I answered. "Of course Frank you'll always be a part of the family. Amanda will probably need you now more than ever."" I choked back the tears as I looked toward the handsome wooden box that would soon be placed in the hearse.

"She still loves you like a father and always will nothing will ever change that." I took Frank into my arms and hugged him close as we both started crying.

CHAPTER 13

Amanda was so devastated by her father's death that we were surprised when she wanted to attend graduation just two days after the funeral. She insisted she had to give her speech now more than ever and spent countless hours rewriting it. We stood proudly as she took her place at the mike, valedictorian of her class.

She smiled out at the class and started with a clear even tone which could be heard by all. "We have spent the last four years preparing ourselves for this day and I am proud to say that I am a member of this class." She waited for the applause to die down then continued. "Tomorrow we will head out in many different directions. Some will go off to colleges across the nation while others will start careers and families right here. I know we will make an impact on the world and hope it will be a positive one." Again the crowd cheered.

She hesitated and looked out over the crowd. Her voice faltered and this time she held on to the podium as she spoke. "I was asked and agreed it would be best not to bring up my parents or their lifestyle, but we were wrong." She again hesitated and looked out over the crowd. "My father was the kindest gentlest man I have ever known and without his guidance and endless tutoring I would probably not be here today."

He could not be with us today because six boys had been taught to hate my father, not because he was a bad man or had done them any harm but because he was gay.

An uneasy silence took hold of the crowd as she continued, "Many say gays should keep their secret in the closet, but my father's death proves it must be brought out into the open. They are not the enemy. They are our neighbors, classmates, and yes even friends and family."

Amanda was in tears and trembling as she finished her speech. "Maybe if more gays could have come out of the closet, my father would not have been killed by the hatred and fear that grows like a weed in the darkness of the unknown." Unable to continue she finished with a muffled . . . "Thank you."

A whisper went through the crowd and then slowly a few people started clapping followed by a few more, a few stood and clapped. It was far from a standing ovation but she had possibly reached a few of them and that was enough for Amanda.

We went on with our lives as best we could. Carl's killers were never found though the incident was highly publicized on the news and in the tabloids.

Even though we spent much of the summer together it was hard to let Amanda go off to college in the fall. I couldn't help noticing how much she looked like her mother when we had met as freshman in college.

It would not be the same with her so far away and I hugged her tightly not wanting to let go. I held her until I felt her pulling away. "Write often," I choked "we're always here if you need anything."

"I know" she replied as she turned to hug her mother. Amanda and Karen's eyes met and filled with tears. "Oh mom," Amanda cried as they embraced. It reminded me of the day Amanda had been born and Karen first held her. It was a connecting with the special bond exists between a mother and daughter. I did not feel left out for I was filled to overflowing with joy at the sight of the two of them together knowing I had been a major part of it all.

We helped her pack the car and stood waving as she drove off down the street. It was hard but we managed to save our tears until she was out of sight and we were alone in the house.

We remembered how exciting it was when we went off to college and wondered if our mothers had felt the emptiness and longing that filled us now.

CHAPTER 14

With Amanda away at college we found ourselves with a lot of time on our hands. Up till now we had gladly spent all our time with Amanda and her many school activities.

The years had passed quickly and both of us had changed in so many ways.

We had drifted into the routine of family life with Amanda as our center. The extra pounds, the touch of gray, and the gentle wrinkles around the mouth and eyes were all reminders that we were not the vibrant young women we had once been.

A month had gone by since Amanda left for college and I watched Karen from behind my newspaper at what had become her morning routine. She was fidgety, pacing back and forth across the room like a caged tigress. Several times she would reach out and touch the lunch box on which Amanda had painted butterflies.

"If you think she needs it, we can take it to her." I smiled.

"Could we?" she beamed at the thought. Her smile quickly fading as she realized I had been kidding.

My smile faded to for I also felt the pain I saw behind those puffy eyes. We had spent so many years building our lives around Amanda that as a couple we had grown apart.

The silence building between us frightened me. We needed to get to know each other again and I would have to do something soon.

Friday when I got off work I had an inspiration. As soon as I got home I asked Karen out on a date.

"A date?" she laughed. "Have you lost your mind?"

"Maybe I have," I put my arms around her "but come on, a night of dinner and dancing will do us both a world of good. Besides it's been ages since we had a night out."

"I think this is a crazy idea," she grinned "but OK. When did you want to go?"

"There's no time like the present."

"Oh no not tonight." she sounded horrified.

"And why not? It's still early." I mused.

"Oh all right if you insist I guess it's better to get it over with." Her lack of enthusiasm almost made me change my mind.

"Let's see what will I wear?" Karen began to sound a little excited by the idea, giving me new hope my plan would succeed.

I was as nervous as I had been the first time we met. I wanted everything to be perfect and was very careful not to let Karen see me take a CD from our collection and slip it in my jacket pocket.

I took her to the same bar near the college where we had met. Not much had changed I thought as we entered the familiar doors from so long ago. The way the girls dressed was the biggest change. The faces still had the same hopeful eyes. Eyes that would search the crowded room hoping to make contact with someone they could share their lives with or at least a small part of it.

We drew a lot of looks from the younger crowd but I was certain this was the place to recapture what I was so afraid we had lost.

We found an empty table near the dance floor much to close to the speakers but I did not plan on staying very long. I left Karen and while getting our drinks slipped by the DJ booth to make my request.

"Don't think we have that one Hun." came her surprised reply.

"I expected it would not be on the play list so brought the CD with me. That is if you don't mind, its song number seven." As I handed her a ten for a tip and the disk I had so carefully hidden from Karen.

"Not at all Hun what's the occasion, if you don't mind my asking?"

"Nothing special, we met here and are just trying to recapture some of the magic from twenty plus years ago."

"Ahhh I see, well don't you worry I'll be more than happy to play it for you." She smiled and winked at me as she turned to change the music which had been playing.

I brought Karen her drink and sat down close to her. I could see she was not happy and the loud speakers where giving her a headache. "We'll go after this drink." I promised.

"No, I'm fine. We can stay." Karen lied terribly.

"Well my head is telling me one drink will be more than enough." I wanted Karen to know she was not the only one to old for music played this loud. She smiled and I could see relief written all over her face.

With the last boom of the speakers from a song that had filled the dance floor, I heard the crackle of someone messing with a mike.

"We have a special request tonight." I heard the DJ's voice boom from the speaker next to us. "This goes out to a couple who met here over twenty years ago."

I was caught off guard by the announcement and became very self-conscious as everyone turned to look at Karen and me. Of course it had to be us we were the only ones in the place old enough to have been together so long.

"You didn't" Karen blushed.

I whispered as I stood. "I asked her to play the song I didn't expect her to make an announcement." I offered Karen my hand and spoke clearly. "My turn to ask, Can I have the pleasure of this dance."

Karen took my hand and followed me to the dance floor. I held her close as we swayed to the same song we had so many years ago. I found the magic of our love still there as I felt the flame flicker and start to grow between us once again. Except for the music the room was silent and all eyes were on us as we danced. When the song finished the DJ's voice once again boomed through the speakers.

"See ladies there really is hope for that forever after kinda love." This brought on a thunderous round of applause and whistles.

I was embarrassed but Karen laughed the same confident laugh that had drawn my attention to her so many years ago. My love was suddenly filled to overflowing, which must have showed on my face for she stopped laughing and gazed into my eyes.

"I love you." I said confident she felt the same.

She pulled me closer. "I love you too, now let's go home."

We gathered our belongings from the table and headed for the door. Many patrons reached out to pat us on the back or shake our hands wishing us, as one bright faced young woman put it continued togetherness.

Caught up in the moment I forgot to retrieve the CD from the DJ. I thought it a small price to pay for helping us rediscover the love we still shared.

Although Amanda was still a big part of our lives we were now able to focus on getting to know one another all over again.

We started doing things we could do together and Karen began to smile more. Something I was beginning to think she had forgotten how to do. In many ways our love was stronger now than it had been before.

With Amanda in college we decided to make a dream of our own come true. We sold the house and bought a few acres just north of Houston with a small house and a nice little pond. It actually took less time for me to get to work because I didn't have to fight my way through the downtown traffic.

We had wanted to do this for years but thought it best for Amanda to stay in one place while she was in school.

After some refresher courses Karen started teaching at the local High School. She loved the students but had forgotten how much work was actually involved. The long nights spent grading papers and preparing the next day's lesson.

We got a few chickens so we could have fresh eggs, planted a small garden and took in half a dozen stray dogs that had found their way to our doorstep. We put up signs for the first three that no one ever claimed.

One day I saw a man pull up with one of our posters in hand. I thought he had come in search of his lost dog. He opened the door of his car but did not get out. I was horrified when he put a small dog out next to the road and then sped away. I was furious as I ran out to the road. I was to late the man was gone and only the tiny brown fur ball remained. Barely a handful, he was a friendly little pup I named rags.

That afternoon I went around and collected all the posters we had so carefully made and put up. Seems they had a hidden message . . . will give unwanted dogs a good home. Regardless of where they came from we loved them all and they were good watchdogs.

We were happy here, quite evenings on the porch, weekends spent fishing or swimming in our own pond.

CHAPTER 15

Amanda finished college and lucky for us had become a veterinarian. She met and married a man who was also a vet and we were looking forward to our first grand baby.

The call came a month earlier than expected at 1:00 am. We dressed quickly and started toward the hospital.

"Slow down." Karen insisted. "It could be hours before anything happens."

It was dark and taking a curve to fast have put many drivers into the ditch so I relented and eased off the accelerator.

When the road straightened and the city lights came into view I pressed down on the pedal a little more. I ran the first light being careful to make sure no cross traffic was coming.

"Lynn!" Karen exclaimed.

She did not need to say anymore. "Sorry with the baby coming so early and all I just want to get there."

"Doctors have been known to get the due date wrong before. I'm sure that's all it is." Karen tried to ease my fears.

"We knew within a week of certainty when Amanda would be born."

"Well dear that was a little different we knew the exact date of conception. It's a little harder to pin point in this case."

I reluctantly stopped for the next light and sure enough we hit the next three red as well. My foot was sitting on the brake but ready to hit the gas as soon as it turned changed to green. "Why is it when you're in a hurry every light is red?"

"Calm down," Karen said as she took my hand in hers and smiled. "After seeing you this way I'm glad you weren't there to drive me to the hospital when Amanda was born."

At the moment I smiled back I heard the sickening sound metal making contact, and felt our car surge forward. I instinctively pressed harder on the brakes and before the reality of what was happening set in I saw I was headed toward the windshield. I closed my eyes anticipating the impact did not come. I was barely an inch from the glass when my seat belt caught and pulled me back toward the seat. While in midair another impact sent me flying sideways. My head hit something and all went black.

I do not think I was unconscious for long because I was still in the car when I opened my eyes. Everything was blurry, and my mouth was so dry. I tried to move my right arm but it would not respond. I raised my left hand and wiped my eyes. When I pulled it away it was covered with blood. My thoughts immediately turned to Karen. I twisted against the pain trying to see where and how she was.

I was horrified to see she was pinned against my right side. My arm was twisted grotesquely with our fingers still intertwined. Her side of the car was totally destroyed. It was impossible to tell where the twisted metal ended and Karen began. Blood was everywhere and she was so pale.

When I looked at her face her eyes were fixed, as if staring out into nothingness.

"Karen" I cried but got no response.

"Karen" I called as loud as I could.

Her eyes blinked as if she were coming back from some far away place. She smiled weakly. "The baby's going to be O.K. Karen Lynn is so beautiful. Give her a kiss for me." She was having trouble breathing.

"Give her a kiss yourself. God damn it!"

"Lynn" she turned to face me as much as she could. "I love you so much."

"Don't you leave me, Karen I need you, the baby needs you, all of us need you. You can't die, you just can't." I was crying as I reached out to wipe away the single tear from her cheek. I somehow knew this would be my last chance to tell her. It was not easy but I held back my tears, "I love you too." and with that said I heard the long exhale of Karen's last breath.

I felt a pain so deep that the physical pain from my injuries seemed nothing. I wanted to scream but no sounds came forth and all I could do is cry.

It was only a few minutes later I felt a hand on my shoulder. "Don't worry we're going to get you out of there."

"I'm O.K. help Karen." I said as a small ray of hope filled my heart.

The young man checked her pulse. "I'm afraid she's gone."

"Nooooo" I howled sounding like the lonely cry of a wolf baying at the moon. "She hasn't been gone that long. You can bring her back I know you can."

"I'm afraid she's lost to much blood." He said matter-of-factly.

"Then give her mine." I screamed, "Anything just save her."

"We'll do what we can" The grim faced young man replied before he started tending to my wounds.

Even though movement caused me great pain I managed to push his hands away. "No her first." I coughed the words out then wiped blood from my mouth.

He looked to Karen then back to me. My head was spinning but I had to hold on. I had to make sure he took care of Karen. I watched as he got an IV ready and then started to prep Karen's arm.

"Mark what have we got here." I heard a harried voice say but everything was getting blurry and I could not see who was speaking.

"Multiple lacerations, looks like some internal injuries and I'm afraid this one is beyond our help." No I thought but could not utter a sound as the darkness once again overtook.

Somewhere in the void of my unconsciousness Karen came to me and took my hand in hers.

"Lynn, Lynn." She called to me.

"Karen."

"Yes I'm here with you. You're going to be all right."

"But I don't want to be all right. I want to be with you."

"You can't my love."

"But why, why can't I come with you."

"Because it's not your time, you must go on."

"Karen." I called out over and over again into the void but she was gone.

"Lynn, Oh Lynn you can't leave us too." Amanda's tearful voice called to me now.

My eyes fluttered open slowly. Amanda was sitting by my side her head resting face down on the bed as she cried. I reached out and gently stroked her hair to which she sat up with a start and our eyes met.

"Don't . . ." I tried unsuccessfully to smile. My mouth dry making it hard to speak but I wanted to calm some of her fears. "Don't worry I . . . . have it . . . on good authority it is not my time yet."

Amanda was laughing and crying at the same time. Her eyes glazed over and her lower jaw trembled, "Mom" was all she could manage before her body shook from the deep sobs that can only be caused by such a deep loss. Her husband, Don came to her side and took her in his arms.

"I . . . know." I cried not wanting to hear the words neither of us could speak.

I had been unconscious for twenty-four hours. Even with three compound fractures and some busted ribs, nothing hurt as much as my heart.

The doctor came in and chased everyone out so he could examine me. "You're a pretty lucky lady." He smiled.

With Amanda out of the room I did not have to hide or sugar coat how I really felt and tears immediately filled my eyes. "I don't feel so lucky."

"Yes, well we expect for you to make a full recovery."

"I don't want to be here without Karen."

"Well your family needs you; they've lost a great deal already."

I knew he meant well, but how could he possibly know what I had lost.

I was grateful when he finished and was gone. I wanted to be alone but Amanda was soon by my side, trying to smile.

After drinking some water I was better able to talk. Still not wanting to speak of what we both knew to be true. I asked. "How's . . . Karen Lynn?"

Amanda seemed surprised by this question. "She's doing fine, but how'd you know we had given her that name."

"Your mother told me." I answered taking another sip of water holding back yet more tears.

Amanda looked at me in disbelief. "But we were expecting a boy and did not choose the name until today."

"We had decided on Jennifer, after dad's mom but when they placed her in my arms the name Karen Lynn filled my thoughts. It was as if she had whispered the name to me and no other would do."

I told her how her mother had seemed so far away and she had said that not the baby was beautiful but Karen Lynn was beautiful. This led us to believe she had really seen the baby and if it were at all possible she was with us now.

The doctors did not want me to leave the hospital for the funeral but gave into my persistence by agreeing it would be ok as long as a registered nurse was in attendance. They rigged a wheel chair so I could not move my legs at all and I had to keep the IV going. It was full of antibiotics to keep my bones from becoming infected from the compound fractures.

I would do anything and pay any amount as long as I could be there.

Roger had taken care of all the arrangements. He and Susan watched over me protectively as people came to pay their last respects and tell us how sorry they were that such a thing could happen.

There were many visitors, even some of her former students came to say goodbye. I was in a daze and all I could do was look at the casket. I did not hear much of what was said and when I did not respond it was explained I was heavily sedated.

I heard the minister from our little church ask if anyone else would like to say something. I shook my head clear. "I would like to say something." Everyone seemed surprised as Susan brought me the mike.

"Karen was my confidant, my friend, and my lover. I miss her dearly." I took some deep breaths closed my eyes in an unsuccessful attempt to hold back the tears. They streamed down my face as I spoke.

I had hoped to be strong for Amanda's sake but I could not. I had to say what was in my heart. "It's not fair." I cried, "It's not." I looked vacantly out at the faces of our friends and relatives. "A lifetime of love is not enough." I took a deep breath between sobs. "It's just . . . not enough." The nurse must have given me some medication for I remember nothing else, not even giving up the mike.

$\mathcal{E}$PILOG

It's been a few years since the accident that took Karen from me. She still visits me in my dreams and at times I can feel her presence in my waking hours.

It is hard at times to deal with the connection but I thoroughly enjoy spending time with our granddaughter Karen Lynn and her little brother Don Jr.

The drunk driver who hit us and pushed us into the path of an oncoming truck was sentenced to five years for vehicular manslaughter. They wanted to go after the truck driver too, something about hours of service. The charges were dropped and I like to think my testimony on his behalf helped make a difference.

Sure there might have been something he could have done differently but then again I could have run the light and not been there, a thought that haunts me all the time. He was just as much a victim of the drunk driver as we had been.

Physically my body has healed. Although I walk with a limp and the doctor thinks I'm crazy because I won't let him operate to restore total feeling to my right hand.

I tell him. "It doesn't hurt, just feels a little numb. It feels like she's still holding my hand."

This worries him. "You need to see a psychiatrist to help you get over the emotional loss."

Let him worry, for I prefer to think our love was just too great to be limited by the boundary of a mere lifetime.